THE ART OF STEALING A DUKE'S HEART

THIEVES OF DESIRE BOOK 1

ELLIE ST. CLAIR

♥ **Copyright 2021 Ellie St Clair**

All rights reserved.

This book or parts thereof may not be reproduced in any form, stored in any retrieval system, or transmitted in any form by any means—electronic, mechanical, photocopy, recording, or otherwise—without prior written permission of the publisher.

Facebook: Ellie St. Clair

Cover by AJF Designs

Do you love historical romance? Receive access to a free ebook, as well as exclusive content such as giveaways, contests, freebies and advance notice of pre-orders through my mailing list!

Sign up here!

Also By Ellie St. Clair

Thieves of Desire
The Art of Stealing a Duke's Heart

For a full list of all of Ellie's books, please see
www.elliestclair.com/books.

CHAPTER 1

LONDON ~ 1812

"You can try as hard as you like, but you will never blend in."

Calliope fixed an annoyed gaze on her sister, who so easily slipped into the shadows unnoticed that Calli hadn't even seen her approach.

"We are supposed to be avoiding one another."

"That's what Arie said, yes, but then Arie isn't here, now is he?"

One corner of Calli's lips tugged up into a smile. Diana was right, but while she had always been the forgotten one, she was also, in her own way, the most rebellious.

While Calli would far prefer to be recognized for proving her worth.

"You're supposed to be searching the house by now," Diana said from the corner of her mouth. "Why are you still here in the ballroom?"

Calli sighed as she turned from her sister, staring out

across the dance floor in front of them, at the swirls of colorful gowns draping the women's bodies, and the dashing gentlemen who held their partners in close embraces.

"I just... wanted to watch the dancing. I've never seen a waltz like this before."

"We learned it, though."

It was true. It had been part of all of their lessons. Lessons on how to be one of these people, how to fit in and make everyone believe their lies.

"But to dance it, here, in such a room, with the angels watching from paintings above, surrounded by white stucco pillars, my feet on marble, it would be like I was dancing among the gods and goddesses themselves."

Diana choked out a bark of laughter at Calli's fanciful words, and Calli found her face growing hot at the fact that she had actually said them aloud.

"This is not your world, Calli. It never will be. We are here for one purpose, and one purpose only. Do you understand?"

Calli gave a quick nod before turning from the scene in front of her. Diana was right. She had a job to do. One she could hardly believe that Arie had actually trusted her with. Calli smoothed her hand down the grey muslin of her skirts, created for this very function. She was to fit in, to make all believe she was a companion, not a debutante who would be expected to be making her acquaintance with young gentlemen or stepping onto the floor in a waltz.

"Besides," Diana said, her voice softening as she stared at the woman who was her sister in nearly every sense of the word, "if you were to step out onto that dance floor, every person — man or woman — would not be able to help but notice you. You would be the talk of Society."

"I would not," Calli said with a roll of her eyes, looking down at her inconspicuous garment. They had swept back all of her riotous black curls, doing their utmost to tame them into a harsh knot at the back of her head, while her face was devoid of anything that might highlight her prominent features.

"You told Arie you could do this," Diana continued. "So are you going to follow through, or not?"

"Of course I am," Calli said, straightening her spine. She was determined to show her brother that she was as capable as any of them at accomplishing success in the family business. "Here I go."

Diana nodded in approval. "I'll keep watch."

Calli slipped through the crowds, closing her eyes for a moment as she reviewed the map of the grand London townhouse in her mind. She would start in the drawing rooms, then move back through the house. She was sure to eventually find her quarry. She just had to make sure she did so unnoticed.

The key to accessing entry, she reminded herself, hearing Arie's words in her head, *is to convince everyone around you that you belong.*

She nodded with a small smile to the maid she passed as she walked through the foyer, and the girl nearly ran away. Calli wondered if she was supposed to remain hidden from the guests.

While each of her siblings possessed their own extraordinary skill, they had all learned the ways of the nobility so that they would fit into their surroundings when the occasion called for it. Calli had never quite grasped the way the upper crust treated those who they considered below them — especially the people who worked for them.

But no matter. That was why she should feel no guilt over what she was about to do.

Besides, if she did her job correctly, no one would ever be

the wiser, and the duke could continue to enjoy his fine artwork.

She cracked open the first door, finding the drawing room ready for visitors, but currently unoccupied. She slipped in, rounding the room and finding plenty of paintings that would fetch a good price, but none that she was looking for.

A parlor and dining room later, she was still without success.

Trying not to panic, reminding herself that she was trained for this and would be just fine, she pushed open the last door before the end of the small corridor.

And found herself swallowed by the darkness of a decidedly masculine room.

While embers still burned in the grate, this room was not ready for visitors, and Calli received the impression more than ever that she was trespassing. She crossed to the desk, where a candle awaited in a surprisingly plain small holder. She lit the wick before lifting it high as she crossed the room, beginning at the door as she made a slow circle, casting the flickering light upon the walls.

This was never going to work, she thought, shaking her head. Even if she found the painting, she would never be able to study it. Not in this light. Most certainly not with enough detail to ever do it justice.

She sighed. She would have to return and tell Arie she had failed. She could already see the disappointment on his face as he sighed and told her that he never should have trusted her. If only there was another way.

Just as Calli was about to turn to the door, color glimmered from across the room, where her light had reflected off a painting on the far wall. Her heart began to drum excitedly in her chest. There it was.

She began to step closer to the painting, the swells of the

sea drawing her, when the door swung open, freezing her footsteps. She closed her eyes, wishing that by doing so she could hide completely, but she was far too old to believe such a thing.

She turned, ever so slowly, waiting to see who had caught her in their trap.

Only to find two blond-haired, blue-eyed children, their cherubic chubby faces seemingly having come to life from the murals in the ballroom, staring at her with grins on their faces.

* * *

This had been a mistake.

Although, so were most of the decisions Jonathan had made in his three decades so far on earth.

None, perhaps, had such serious repercussions as the throwaway promise he had made to his sister.

"Of course, I'll look after them," he had said when she had asked if he would take care of her twin children if anything were to ever happen to her. "I wouldn't expect you to trust any other more than your brother."

At the time, he had never expected that his exuberant, carefree sister was actually planning her own departure, that she was leaving her children, already devoid of a father who had died too young, for a life of adventure. It still caused rage to rise within him every time he remembered reading the note. The note that explained she was running away to America, but that it was too much to take her children. That she was never meant to be a mother, and would Jonathan please look after them?

Jonathan's own mother had been so beside herself that Jonathan was left arranging their care alone. He had hired the best of governesses, determined to provide them a home and a proper education, but knew nothing more of what he was to do.

But now, his mother was insisting that the children required a mother figure. This ball was supposed to help him find one. Of course, his mother herself, who far preferred Bath, had not even bothered to attend, but that was actually for the better.

For the thought of tying himself to one of these women for the rest of his life made him ill. None of them seemed capable of becoming a mother as most of the young ladies vying for his attention were little more than children themselves. And the twins were not exactly the most... docile of creatures.

Speaking of the little hellions...

He caught a glimpse of a blond head from across the ballroom, and it was not the elaborately coiffed hair of one of the young ladies. No, this was wild, bouncing blond hair that was running away after being caught somewhere it didn't belong.

"Damn it," he said, his grip on his glass so strong he nearly crushed it.

"Everything all right, Hargreave?"

Belatedly, Jonathan remembered his friend, Davenport, who was standing beside him, surveying the room in front of him with a smirk on his face. He had always been the carefree sort, a trait that Jonathan envied. For Jonathan cared all too much.

"Fine," he said tersely, knocking back his drink before setting it on the empty tray of a passing servant. "I must go attend to something."

"Would that 'something' be a precocious six-year-old?"

Jonathan eyed him sharply. If Davenport had seen either of the children, then he couldn't be sure who else had witnessed their presence.

"They must have outwitted Mrs. Blonsky again," he said with a sigh. "She told me she couldn't keep up. I should have listened to her."

"Why do you have your housekeeper watching them?" Davenport asked, one of his black eyebrows lifted.

"The new governess failed to arrive this morning."

"How many is that now?"

Jonathan eyed him sharply, sensing the amusement in his friend's voice. But this was no laughing matter. He had spent far too many hours hiring governesses and then listening to their complaints as they quit. He was through with it. At least a wife wouldn't be able to leave the situation.

Davenport was still waiting for an answer.

"Six." Jonathan muttered.

"Six! One a month, then."

"So it is. Excuse me."

He set out of the ballroom, hoping that the little monkeys hadn't invaded the dance floor, but were somewhere on the periphery. Not sensing them or any commotion made by them in the big room, he continued through the ground floor of the house, observing each room as he went, interrupting one scandalous affair that he basically ignored before moving on.

Perhaps the children had actually returned to the nursery, or Mrs. Blonsky had found them, he considered hopefully, already knowing that either idea was too good to be true.

A peal of laughter confirmed that.

He hurried down the corridor to the study, his mind already running over all the kinds of trouble they could find themselves in. He tried to remember if he had locked his desk drawers. He was sure he had, and even if they did manage to break into his ledgers and destroy them, his man-of-business had another set, but still… there was only one man Jonathan *completely* trusted.

Himself.

Annoyed at the dismal affair, the disappearing governess, and the fact that his niece and nephew couldn't even give him one night in which they would stay out of trouble, he was not entirely subtle when he pushed open the door, stepping through the opening with determination to end this madness and demonstrate to his niece and nephew exactly what happened when they disobeyed.

Only to find himself momentarily speechless.

For there, sitting demurely in front of the two chairs before his desk, were two little angels, gazing raptly, silently — for once — at the woman before them.

She spoke with exuberance, her hands flying in front of her, her face full of expressions as she spoke of animals and goddesses and nonsense tales.

The children seemed to be enjoying every minute of it.

So much so, that they hadn't even noticed him. Not yet.

Until suddenly, the woman stopped mid-sentence before turning toward him with her hands still lifted, her mouth rounded in an O.

After the moment in which she was seemingly suspended in time, she threw back the chair so quickly she nearly knocked it over before running a few steps backward.

"My lord, I'm so very sorry, I—"

"Your Grace."

"Pardon me?" Her cheeks flushed a most becoming shade of red.

"The correct address for a duke is 'Your Grace.'"

"Yes, Your Grace, of course. My apologies. I did not mean to sit in your chair, it was just that the children told me they were not tired, and I thought perhaps I would tell them a bedtime story. It always used to help me, although ideally they would actually be in their beds and—"

Jonathan took a breath, closing his eyes for a moment as he held up a hand to quell her flow of words.

"You are late, Miss Donahue."

"Pardon me?" she said again, her eyes wide, revealing the most stunning shade of violet-blue he had ever seen.

"I said that you are late. You are Miss Donahue, are you not?"

"I… Y-yes."

"Very well. Welcome. Not only are you late, but you have arrived in the middle of a house party, and you are entertaining the children from my chair in my study. But, if you happen to suit with the children, all of that will be overlooked."

"I—what?" She looked at him in surprise, and he wondered if most employers were stricter. Perhaps he would have to rectify that issue.

"Children," he said to the twins, "meet your new governess."

CHAPTER 2

Calli swallowed hard. *Governess?* Surely he must be joking. She had agreed, for she had no idea how else to explain her presence in his study, but she had immediately regretted doing so.

She looked down at the two children in front of her, whose smiles had somehow become wicked gleams at the words from their—father?

Panic rose in her breast as she tried to remember what Arie had said, to assume an air of self-assurance. She tried to focus on the man — the *duke's* — actual words.

He assumed her to be a late-arriving governess. Which meant… that she now had an opportunity. An opportunity to study the painting in question in detail. An opportunity to, if she was able to find the time and the right place, paint it to her liking and check it against the original. An opportunity to make her family proud.

She forced a smile onto her face, looking up at the man who wore his handsomeness with an arrogance she found rather off-putting. But she supposed that's what came with being a duke.

"My apologies for my lateness, Your Grace," she said, attempting sincerity. "I had… travel trouble. And then when I arrived to see the house party, I was unsure of whether to enter and meet with you, so I was awaiting you here when the children found me."

It sounded like a perfectly plausible explanation… didn't it?

"I would suggest that the best place to tell the children a bedtime story would be in their nursery."

"Uncle, it's not a nursery," the boy said, the edge of a whine in his voice. "That is for children, and we are not children anymore."

"What would you have me call it, then, Matthew?"

"The schoolroom and our bedroom," he said with a nod of his head that was so confident it made Calli smile. Uncle, he had called this duke. Whatever had happened to these children's parents?

"Very well. Up you go. In the absence of Mrs. Blonsky, wherever she may be, would you please show Miss Donahue up to her own room?"

"Of course, Uncle," the little girl said, a gleam in her eye that Calli wasn't entirely sure of. The truth was, she had very little experience with children, as she and her siblings were all rather close to the same age. They couldn't be particularly difficult to deal with, though… could they?

"To her *actual room*, Mary," the duke said sternly, and Calli began to suspect that the children were not always as well-behaved as it might first seem. She bit her lip as she stared at the two of them, wondering if she had gotten herself into something she might not be able to handle.

"I must first go retrieve my bag, Your Grace," she said with what must have been the clumsiest of curtsies. She had never been able to completely get it right.

"Where would your bag be, Miss Donahue?" he asked dryly.

"Tucked away near the front entrance," she said. "I shall be but a moment."

"What of the children?" he asked, one of his dark eyebrows raised.

Calli smoothed her hands down her skirts nervously. "What of them?"

"Who will watch them while you go retrieve your bag?"

"Umm…" Couldn't he do it? It somehow didn't seem entirely appropriate to ask, however. "I shall go later, then?"

"Very good," he said, seemingly relieved. "Please meet me here in my study at one o'clock tomorrow afternoon, and we will review all of the particulars."

She nodded, unable to keep herself from noticing the vivid blue of his eyes that seemed to bore right into her, seeing altogether too much.

"Yes, Your Grace."

"I best return to my party," he said, but despite his words he made no actual move to the door, instead his gaze lingering on her, from the top of her head down to the borrowed slippers that were poking out from beneath her dress. "Welcome, Miss Donahue."

"Thank you," she practically whispered, so thrown was she by his perusal. She wanted to rage against his arrogance, that he could view her as some doxy to be so entirely objectified, but he was a duke — and now, her employer. Of a sort.

And then there was the fact that his stare left not just annoyance but also… a tingling that she didn't know, nor didn't want, to give name to. A tingling that wanted to know more of who he was and what he might think of her.

Which was ridiculous, she told herself, as she hurried the children out of the room, studiously avoiding this man's gaze. They were down the hall and up the stairs before the children turned to her and began to talk, spinning what she already knew were tall tales.

"You sleep in the attic," Mary said primly. "By yourself. Except for the ghost, of course."

"Of course," Calli murmured, doing her best to keep her twitching lips from curling up into a smile. "And is that where your bedrooms are as well?"

"No," Matthew said, with a shake of his head. "Ours are on the second floor."

"Do you sleep alone, then?" she asked, raising her eyebrows at them in mock horror. "Who is to protect you?"

"We don't need protection," Mary said, crossing her arms over her chest.

"You don't?" Calli said, placing one hand on a hip, the other over her mouth as though she was properly horrified. "But what if the baddies come in the night?"

"The baddies?" Both children said in unison.

"Yes — the monsters that form from the dust under your beds and come to take revenge on the boys and girls who have created them!"

The children — who Calli considered must be twins — exchanged a glance at that.

"You are making up a story," Matthew said, his bottom lip pouting out as he seemed entirely displeased.

"You are right," Calli said, relenting. "I am."

"Why would you do that?" Mary asked, her anger now overcoming the fear she had been trying to hide.

"Why did you make up a story for me?"

"Because… because we wanted to play a trick on you!" Mary responded.

"I know. And how did it feel to be on the other side of that?"

"I—" Mary began, exchanging a look with Matthew, but neither of them seemed to have an answer for her. "We'll show you to your room," she said, pouting as she began down the second floor corridor. Calli smiled in satisfaction. Perhaps she had this handled after all.

Mercifully, the children fell asleep rather quickly, and Calli was soon creeping back downstairs, looking up and down each corridor to make sure that no one saw her sneaking about the house. The staff would soon recognize her as the governess, and she had to make sure that she wasn't tied to a guest at the event. She thanked the heavens when she saw Diana outside of the ballroom, her face screwed up in concern as she was apparently looking for Calli.

"Diana!" Calli hissed from around the corner. "Diana!"

Diana's head turned at her name, and she hurried toward Calli, grabbing her hand and rushing them into one of the small rooms, which seemed to be a parlor.

"Where have you been?" Diana exclaimed.

"Well, I found the painting," Calli said, as hurriedly as she could. "But I found something else as well. As soon as I found it in the study, the door opened and two children came in."

"Children?"

"Yes, children. It seems they are the niece and nephew of the duke. They began to question me about who I was and what I was doing there, but I was able to evade their inquisition and turned it around on them. Soon enough, I was telling them a story — one that Arie always told us when we were younger — and then the next thing I knew, the duke walked in!"

Diana gasped. "He didn't."

"He did." Calli nodded grimly. "And he took me to be the new governess."

"Oh, Calli," Diana groaned. "You weren't supposed to get yourself noticed."

"Well, too late for that," Calli said with a shrug. "I decided, however, that it might actually be of benefit. It will give me time to study this painting, to complete my own version to my liking. By the time I am finished, we can switch them out and no one will be the wiser."

"Are you sure about this?" Diana asked, her worry evident. "We all have our skills, you know. Yours is your painting, we all know that. But as to your level of deception…"

"I'll be fine," Calli said with a wave of her hand. They were always doubting her, and she was sick of it. She was going to prove that she could handle this — *all* of this — and for once, be the hero of the family. "But I do need your help."

"Of course."

"I need you to retrieve a bag for me — quickly, as I said it was here, in the house. I'll need some dresses, ones that are passable as a governess but nothing that is particularly pretentious. All the essentials as well as my oil paints — the ones that Xander mixed for me. You know what to bring. Meet me at the servant's entrance in two hours' time."

Diana nodded. "Very well. And what shall I tell Arie?"

"The truth."

* * *

AND SO, two hours later, Calli was crouched down outside of the servants' entrance, shivering as she waited for her sister to arrive, hoping once more that she would attract no notice.

It was dark back here, a few hedgerows separating the mews from the front green.

A figure approached in the dark, but as it neared, Calli soon realized that it wasn't her sister after all, but rather one of her brothers. Despite knowing she should stay in the shadows, she couldn't help herself from jumping up and running to Xander — the only one of her siblings who was so by blood and not by the assumed family they had formed.

"Xander!" she said, wrapping her arms around him, relieved at the opportunity to be able to talk to him. "What are you doing here?"

"Arie sent me instead of Diana," he said in a hushed voice, pulling Calli back into the shadows. "He didn't think she should be out again alone."

"It is my fault she had to return alone in the first place," Calli muttered, wondering if this entire scheme was ridiculous.

"She told us what happened. I think it was rather quick of you to go along with everything."

"Thank you," Calli said, lighting up a bit inside at the praise. "What did Arie say?"

The head of their family was one of their toughest critics, though he also loved them all more than anyone else ever would.

Xander hesitated. "At first, he was upset."

"I knew he would be."

"Only because he was worried about you," Xander added. "Then he began to see the merits of the idea."

"Good," Calli said, letting out the breath she didn't even know she had been holding. "And what do you think?"

"I think that it would be rather interesting to stay and watch you in the role of a governess," Xander said with a laugh, and even though it was dark, Calli could picture the twinkle in his eye. "However, my job is to watch you from a distance, make sure you are all right. How long do you think this painting will take you?"

Calli frowned. "It is more detailed than I thought, and while I do have a private room, it connects to the children's, which will make finding time difficult. I shall have to do it at night, once everyone is asleep. It could take a few weeks."

Weeks away from her family, in a strange house, with children who she had a feeling were not going to make life easy for her.

"You can do it," Xander said encouragingly, and she was suddenly most worried about what it was going to like to be away from her brother. "If you need anything, just look for me. I'll be close."

Calli took the bag from his outstretched hand, then reached in to give him one last embrace.

"Thank you, Xander."

"I have faith in you, Calli."

CHAPTER 3

Jonathan woke the next day in the foulest of moods.

He kept his eyes closed even as his valet opened the curtains, trying to remember what had caused his ire.

There was the party, which, while many would have called it a success, his mother would consider a failure for he had not danced — not even once. None of the women were enticing enough, nor promising enough to attract his attention, and he certainly had no wish to lead on any woman who might be holding out hope to be his bride.

And then—oh yes, and then.

There *had* been one woman whom he had considered with more than a passing glance. A woman with red, rosy lips that stretched into an all-too-enticing smile. One certainly too enticing for a governess. A woman with a beauty mark that drew attention to the most peculiar violet-blue eyes which widened in an innocence that his niece and nephew were going to take advantage of in no time at all. A woman whose form was too curvy in all the right places, with hips that invited him to cup, breasts that were far too pert and welcoming, and a waist he wanted to span with his hands.

The governess. The woman who would now be living in the same house as him, tempting him, taunting him, when she was supposed to be keeping the children from destroying his life.

Once she had stood from his desk and he had gotten a good look at her, he had been tempted to tell her to turn around and leave. He knew, however, that it might be difficult to find another governess, and he was in a rather tight spot already. But he had enough to worry about without a siren under his roof, most especially a siren who didn't seem to understand the proper protocols in the house of a duke.

Such as not sitting in his chair. Not entering his study without permission. And not suggesting that *he* watch the children as though he was a nursemaid himself.

The memory of her cheeks turning a most endearing shade of red did summon forth the ghost of a smile, however, and that was when his valet, Oxford, greeted him.

"Tea, Your Grace?"

"Very well," he said, rubbing his eyes. "What time is it?"

"Eleven o'clock, Your Grace."

Two hours, then, until his meeting with the governess. He should have Mrs. Blonsky do it. But then, Mrs. Blonsky had made it clear she wanted as little to do with the children as possible. He sighed and squared his shoulders. Best to do this himself.

* * *

CALLI'S BROTHER had prepared her for many circumstances that might arise from her foray within the nobility. He had not, however, foreseen that she just might become a governess.

Which meant that she had no idea just what, exactly, she was supposed to do with these two children.

Breakfast took up the first hour — which, they told her, they *never* ate with their uncle.

Afterward, they sat around the small round table in the corner of the nursery with its rather blank walls that Calli felt required much more adornment, looking at one another with open curiosity.

"How often do you see him?" Calli asked, trying not to appear overly curious, as she wondered just what the relationship was between these children and their standoffish uncle. He didn't seem particularly interested in them.

Matthew shrugged. "Sometimes for dinner."

"But not often," Mary added. "He doesn't like us much."

"What are you talking about?" Calli exclaimed. "Of course he likes you!"

Mary snorted, her expression advanced beyond her years. "You don't know him. He doesn't like children, and he wishes he'd had nothing to do with us. He's still mad at Mother for leaving us."

"Oh, I'm sure she had no choice," Calli said, her heart opening to these children, knowing that their mother must have passed in order for them to have been left alone.

"She did," Mary said with a curt nod of her head, her blond hair dancing around her chin as she did so. "She ran off to America. Her new husband didn't want us, so she left us behind."

Calli stared at them, speechless.

"No…"

"Yes," Matthew said with such emphasis that Calli realized how deep the children's scars must be right now. "But it's fine. We have each other. Right, Mary?"

"Right," she said with a small smile, and if Calli's heart wasn't already aching for these children, it began bleeding anew. They may not feel wanted, but whatever time she was going to be spending here, she would show them that they were worth something, that she enjoyed their company.

As long as they never found out her true reason for being here.

"What would you like to do today?" she asked, perhaps overly brightly.

"We don't have to do any schooling?" Mary asked, her eyes widening hopefully.

"Not today," Calli said, shaking her head. She would have to figure out that aspect of her job here — sometime between actually caring for these children and painting. "Let's do something fun."

"Go to the park?" Matthew asked, and Calli nodded.

"A fine idea, for later in the day after I meet with your uncle."

"Do you think Uncle would come with?" Mary asked in a small voice, her gaze on the table, and Calli shrugged.

"Perhaps," she said, although she had a good idea just what the duke would say to the suggestion. "I shall ask him. I cannot make any promises, though. Even if he would like to come, there is a good chance he might be busy."

"He's always busy," Matthew said, with forced bravado in his voice.

"Your uncle is an important man," Calli said carefully. "Now, come. We have a couple of hours until I must meet with your uncle. Until then, we shall play a game."

"What kind of game?"

"What kind do you like?"

"Charades?"

"Very well," she said with a smile. "Let's do it."

* * *

"Enter," Jonathan called at the light knock on the door.

Miss Donahue stepped into his study at his call, but he didn't look up as he kept his eyes on the ledger before him. He was reviewing his stock in the shipping company in which he had recently invested. Many men of his station refused to sully their hands or their money in trade, but Jonathan didn't see why he shouldn't invest his funds to grow them further. It would only help the entirety of the estate.

He remained so focused in part because he didn't want to rest his eyes upon this new governess until she was sitting down, so he wasn't tempted once more by the luscious curves he knew she possessed. Hopefully today she was wearing something that did much more to hide what was beneath.

Sensing her presence hovering next to his desk — a scent of honeysuckle suddenly invading and nearly overwhelming him — he found he had no choice but to look up.

"Please sit."

She did as he bid, and he tried to keep himself from too openly appraising her, as difficult as it may be.

Her hair today was much looser, tendrils of curls escaping the chignon at the back of her head to wave around her face. He guessed that she had help preparing herself yesterday, and struggled now to tame what looked to be a wild mane. He wondered if it was any sort of reflection on her own personality. Would she be a difficult woman to employ?

The thought of wild abandon brought altogether wicked thoughts to his mind, which he pushed away as quickly as he could. That was not why this woman was here.

Jonathan was not a rake of any sort, although he was not

a saint either. Why this woman caused such notions to fill his head, he had no idea.

Today she wore a dress of navy blue, as demure as the gown she'd worn yesterday, yet somehow it highlighted the color of her eyes and accented her cheekbones.

"You wished to speak to me?" she said, her smooth, rich voice filling the silence, and Jonathan cursed himself for losing control. The woman must have bewitched him last night for him to be acting such a way.

"Yes," he said with a nod, finding a sheet of paper on the corner of his orderly desk. "Here you will find your salary for each week. I am sure it will meet with your approval. You have every Sunday evening off to do as you please. The children are expected to learn reading, writing, arithmetic, history, geography, and general etiquette. You will teach them accordingly. They are to remain in the second story unless invited to the ground floor. If you are required elsewhere, Mrs. Blonsky can look after them for brief moments of time. Do you have any questions?"

Expecting none, he returned to his ledgers, only to hear her clear her throat expectantly.

"Yes?" He raised his eyes to her once more, making it apparent that he had other things to do than continue with this meeting.

"Where do the children dine?"

"Primarily in the nursery."

"What if they would like to dine with you?"

"I don't often dine with the children."

"Yes," she persisted, "but what if they would like to?"

"I will request their presence when necessary," he said through clenched teeth.

"Very well," she said, with a sigh that was obviously supposed to portray her resignation. "Am I permitted to take them on outings?"

"Of course," he said, "as long as it is somewhere respectable and a groom and a footman accompany you."

"What of their parents?" she asked, catching him off guard.

"What of them?"

"You never told me the situation of how the children came to be here. I think it is important if I am to understand how to teach them."

"You teach them subjects, Miss Donahue, not about their family."

"Yes, but—"

"Their father died when they were but a year old in a shooting accident. Their mother left them last year."

"So it is true, then," she murmured, and when he met her gaze he was shocked to find it full of such sadness.

"You already knew the story?" he asked, his ire growing at the fact she was making him talk about such things.

"They told me, but I couldn't believe such a thing," she said. "A mother not wanting her children?"

"I suppose you were blessed with a doting mother," he said, his voice laced with smoky tension that was supposed to warn her off.

She either didn't hear or didn't care.

"No, actually, my mother died when I was young," she said. "I would have given anything for more time with her."

"Oh," Jonathan said awkwardly, unsure of just how to respond to that. "I am most sorry for your loss."

She waved a hand in the air, and Jonathan couldn't help but notice how much her gestures spoke for her. "It was a long time ago," she said. "Besides, my brother and I were taken in by another... family, and I am as close to them as I could ever imagine being to my true family."

"Very good," he said curtly. "Well, if we are done here—"

"I actually have one more question."

He didn't bother to attempt to hide his annoyance any longer. "Yes, Miss Donahue?"

The sooner this woman and her generous curves, captivating eyes, and plump lips that were practically begging to be kissed if only so she would stop talking, left his study, the better off he would be.

"The children have requested to spend some time with you. What should I tell them?"

He stared at her incredulously. "You are telling me that the first day you begin working for me, they are already bored of your company?"

She flushed in a most arousing manner.

"I don't believe they are sick of my company, Your Grace, but they would like to get to know their uncle. I don't believe this is the first they have brought up the matter, but perhaps no governess before me has brought forward their request."

Not bloody likely. Most governesses seemed to know their place and understood that it was their job to keep the children entertained and not begging for their uncle — a duke with far more important things to keep him busy — to spend time with them.

"If I ever have a moment, Miss Donahue, I will be sure to come check on them as well as on your performance," best to keep her on her toes, "however, you must understand that I am a very busy man and I do not have time to be running around the nursery."

Properly chastised, she dropped her hands to her lap, although he didn't miss the flash in her eyes as she did so, and he wondered whether she was fighting back a retort. He didn't care what she thought, but he did hope she understood when to keep those thoughts to herself.

"Understood, Your Grace."

"Good," he said, standing now so that she had no choice but to do the same. "I have a prior engagement. You may go."

She nodded and walked to the door, and Jonathan had to swallow a groan at the way her hips swayed back and forth with each step. She surely couldn't be doing this on purpose just to torture him — could she?

Grateful she was actually leaving, he let out the breath he had been holding, but found that he was to be disappointed.

"Your Grace?" she called back over her shoulder after cracking open the door, and he couldn't help but notice the long strands of black curls that were now falling from the pins at the back of her head.

"*Yes*, Miss Donahue?" he said tersely.

"Would you like me to meet with you to provide you with updates on the children's progress?"

"No. Just don't quit, and all else will be fine," he muttered, knowing that her suggestion was a good one, but unable to manage the thought of spending another moment alone in her presence.

"Very well, Your Grace," she said, turning back around. "I won't."

With that, the door clicked shut behind her, and she was finally, blessedly, gone.

CHAPTER 4

If Calli didn't have an ulterior motive for staying at this house, she most assuredly would have been gone by now. It was no wonder all the other nannies and governesses had quit. The problem was not, in her opinion, the children, but the man himself, who was too pretentious for words.

She was still practically shaking in her fury when she relieved the maid who was watching the children during her short and pointless meeting with the duke.

"Well?" she said, hands on her hips as she looked down at them, already sick of these four walls that closed them in. "What would the two of you like to do this afternoon?"

"Go to the park?" Mary asked hopefully, to which Calli nodded.

"Very well," she said. "To the park we will go."

They looked at her expectantly, their faces full of hope and innocence, and Calli felt renewed heartbreak for them.

"Let's find our cloaks and gloves, then, shall we?"

She stepped into her room and picked up her cloak, but before she could swirl it around her and place it over her shoulders, a frog jumped out and stared at her with a loud "ribbit," before jumping away.

Calli stared at it in shock, then turned to find two faces peering at her from the doorway, expressions filled with amusement, guilt, and, at the edge, a very small helping of fear.

She lifted her eyebrows at them, looked at the frog, and then, she couldn't help it.

She started to laugh.

The children stared at one another in amazement before turning their gazes toward her as though she had gone mad.

"Ah, Miss Donahue?" Mary said hesitatingly, "why are you laughing?"

"Why, at your joke," she said, deciding the best way to handle this was to do the last thing they would expect. "It was meant to be funny, was it not?"

"Well, yes," Mary said, her brows furrowing. "But not to you."

"How was I supposed to react, then?"

When Mary said nothing, Matthew jumped in. "You were supposed to scream and run away, and then go talk to Uncle and tell him that you are leaving."

Calli sobered and nodded her head thoughtfully. "I see. You do not like me, then? You wish for a new governess?"

Now the children were speechless, and Calli quickly realized what the issue was.

"Or were you hoping at some point that your uncle would grow tired of hiring governesses and spend more time with you himself?"

They hung their heads and refused to look at her.

Calli crouched down to their height to look them in the eye.

"Your uncle is a busy man," she said, frowning as she realized she was only echoing his own words to her, "but when he has the time, he would love to spend it with you."

"He never has the time," Matthew said, kicking the toe of his shoe into the floor.

"He will," Calli said, determined to ensure that she was not making an empty promise. "Now, let's take this frog outside where he belongs, shall we?"

"Are we still going to the park, then?" Mary asked hopefully, and Calli considered the request for a moment before shaking her head.

"We will go outside to the green, but you've lost the chance to go to the park today. Perhaps tomorrow."

They sighed but didn't argue as they gathered their cloaks and trudged out the door.

Calli stooped and picked up the frog, capturing it between her palms as she followed them down the stairs.

Her gaze was on her hands as the frog jumped around within them, rapidly trying to free himself, when they stopped on the first floor landing.

"Let's take the shortest way out," Calli decided, knowing that would be the front door. "Then you can direct me to the closest pond."

"Very well, Miss—" Matthew began, but then was cut off, and Calli furrowed her brow as she looked up to see just what could have caught his attention.

She swallowed hard when she found herself staring into the white linen shirt that was stretching over a wide torso, the muscles nearly visible from where she stood.

"Miss Donahue," his voice, that silky baritone that seemed reserved for her and her alone, did not have the short clipped words that he used when speaking to everyone else. When he said her name, it was almost like a caress.

He was clad in shirt, cravat, and waistcoat, having divested himself of his jacket at some point in the day.

"Your Grace," she practically squeaked.

"Whatever do you have there?"

"Nothing, Your Grace," she said, quickly shaking her head as she stepped around him. "Just something the children and I are placing outside, is all."

"I see," he said, staring after her, and she could practically feel his eyes boring into her back.

The children quickly followed her, obviously, despite their wish that she tell their uncle she was quitting, not wanting her to share the full details of their practical joke.

"This way, Miss Donahue," Matthew said, pulling open the door, and she rushed outside, allowing the door to shut behind her.

Except it didn't. It was caught in a firm hand, and she realized belatedly that the duke had followed them out.

"Your Grace?" she asked, turning to look at him, wondering just what he was doing.

"Your secrets have intrigued me, Miss Donahue," he said wryly.

Calli swallowed hard at the thought of what she was truly keeping from him.

"Please, do lead on."

She wished she could tell him to turn around and re-enter the house, but she was in no position to tell him to do anything at all, let alone anything of the sort.

Instead, they made a small, strange party as they trudged across the lawn to the small pond that Calli had seen from her bedroom window.

Both Calli and the children couldn't help sneaking looks back at the broody, scowling duke who seemed to belong anywhere else on this massive London home but the green in front of it.

The frog croaked and the children attempted to keep in

their laughter, while even Calli let out an unladylike snort in an attempt to hold back her mirth.

"Are you all right, Miss Donahue?" the duke asked, and she nodded. "Fine," she said, choking back the laughter that threatened to remain unchecked.

"Where are we going?" he asked from behind them, and Calli managed, "the pond," in as ordinary of voice as she could accomplish, though she didn't look back for his reaction.

Finally, they arrived, and Calli was dismayed to find the pond was not much of a pond at all, but primarily a form of ornamentation on the large green lawn. Water trickled from a stone font above and a few small hedges surrounded the one side, but there was little place for the frog to call home.

"Is this where he belongs?" Calli whispered to children, wondering how they had ever gotten their hands on such a thing.

"No," Mary whispered back, shaking her head. "He was from the kitchen."

Calli swallowed hard at that, reminding herself to always ask before sampling anything on her plate.

"Well, perhaps he can still be happy here," she said with a shrug as she knelt and released her passenger. He gave one more throaty gurgle before splashing merrily into the water, happy to be free of the trap of her hands and what would have most assuredly been his place on the dinner table.

"Was that a *frog*?" the duke asked, incredulity in his voice from behind them, and Calli forced herself to turn and face him with chin held high.

"It was, Your Grace."

"And just why, Miss Donahue, were you carrying a frog through my house and across my lawn?"

"Well," she began as diplomatically as she could, even as she felt Mary's small hand touch the back of her leg through her dress in a silent plea for her to keep the secret. Which, Calli supposed, was fair, for she was keeping enough lofty secrets of her own from the duke. "The frog somehow found his way into my cloak. I decided I'd best return him to a place where he could be most comfortable."

"I see," said the duke, missing nothing, his eyes roaming from his niece to his nephew. "And no one has any idea how it got there?"

"No, Your Grace," Calli lied.

"Miss Donahue," he said, his voice laced with warning, but Calli forced herself to stand her ground and not back up an inch, "I do not like it when people lie to me. Most especially my employees."

"I understand, Your Grace."

"See that you do," he said, and Calli knew that he meant every menacing tone within his words. "Now, I think I have had enough exploring outdoors today. Good day to all of you."

"Good day, Uncle," the children said in unison.

He began his long, purposeful stride back across the green toward the house. As soon as he was out of earshot, the three of them burst into laughter.

* * *

Jonathan couldn't have said what had compelled him to follow Miss Donahue and the children. There was something about that impish grin on her face that told him she was up to no good — even though he would usually suspect it was the children who were into some kind of mischief or another. When he had realized she was hiding something, his curiosity had become tinged with suspicion. He didn't like when people hid things from him — even if it was something as innocent and yet altogether surprising as a frog.

A frog.

He snorted now even to think of it. It wasn't the first time such a creature had found its way into the upper floors of his house. Of course, the last governess who had discovered one upon her bed sheets had gone screeching through the hallways until the servants had to inform him of the ruckus. Had she not quit on the spot, he would have fired her anyway.

He did not condone the children's actions, but it was the duty of the governess to discipline the children, not to behave like one of them.

Miss Donahue, at least, had passed that test.

She still struck him as all wrong for a governess. When his friend, Collins, had recommended the woman, he certainty didn't recall him mentioning anything about how… fetching Miss Donahue was.

But then, Collins had been married for years, and not only that, was in love with his wife, so maybe he hadn't noticed.

Jonathan strode to the window of his study, unable to keep himself from looking out at the green beyond, watching Miss Donahue and the children run about playing some game. He would prefer that they were a little less boisterous, but he had already involved himself enough in the children's affairs for one day. Besides, who was he to talk, having already traipsed around the green in his shirtsleeves.

His man-of-business knocked on the door, and Jonathan waved him in before retaking his seat behind his desk.

He had much more important things to attend to.

CHAPTER 5

When the children were finally asleep, Calli grasped her sketchpad and pencil in hand. Who would have thought that two six-year-olds could so stubbornly hold off bedtime? She had told them story after story which had been recounted to her by her eldest brother, tales he had brought with him from his own childhood in Greece long ago.

Unfortunately, these two children had been far too intrigued by stories of Artemis and Apollo, and Calli had nearly fallen asleep before they did. She was exhausted after a full day with them, and while she stared longingly at her bed, it would be some time before she could wrap herself in its comforts.

She had work to do.

Unfortunately, most of that work was going to require her to be sneaking around the house. She could only hope that the master was either abed or out somewhere. Calli herself wasn't one to typically take to bed early, but then, she was also not used to chasing after children all day. She could only hope that the duke was like most of the nobility and spent his evenings out carousing or gambling or drinking or whatever it was men like he did.

Although the thought of him taking part in any activity that would require a crack in his otherwise stern and scowling demeanor caused her lips to curl up in a smile. He wasn't exactly one who evoked images of passionate trysts or midnight rendezvous. Although sometimes, when she caught him looking at her in a certain way…

She placed her ear now against the door of his study, hoping that the lack of light visible from underneath the door meant that it was currently unoccupied. Why did this painting have to be in the one room that she most assuredly should not find herself in?

She clutched the doorknob and ever so slowly turned it, poking her head in to find with relief that she was the only one present. She crept in, wishing that she had thought to wrap a shawl around her shoulders, not anticipating how cold the room would be with only embers in the hearth instead of a blazing fire.

No matter.

The original plan had been to make a quick sketch of the painting during the ball last night. Now, she had much more time, but just as much pressure to work as quickly as she could. One never truly knew how much opportunity she would have.

She moved one of the chairs over in front of the painting, taking some time to study and appreciate it before she placed her pencil to paper. It truly was a masterpiece, and a niggle of doubt began to tug at her conscience that she would be able to properly re-create such a wonder, and whether or not she actually should.

She knew her brother Arie would sell the original, although to whom and for what, she had no idea. She never asked just what his intentions were — it wasn't her place to do so nor did she actually want to know.

No, her job was to repay her brother for everything he had done for her — providing her a home, family, food in her belly, and work that didn't require her to sell herself.

Finally, realizing the hour was growing late, Calli got to work. She began with the center of the painting, the ship as it turned with the storm, the fishermen who tried to regain control, and the one man at peace right in the center of it. She became lost in her work, sketching the masts, the rigging, before moving onto the nuances of the sea below and the sky above. She nibbled at her lip even as her fingers and toes grew cold, as the light of the room dimmed, the candle she had used to guide her way down the only brightness now that the fire in the hearth had been reduced to embers. Even her candle was beginning to flicker, and she looked over, startled to see that it had nearly burned down. That showed her what came of using a tallow candle. Yet she couldn't bring herself to use one of her employer's more expensive wax candles for the job she was currently doing, one that would only steal from him.

"A few measurements, then," she murmured, standing and muttering to herself as she made small marks and notes on her paper to make sure that she had this right. She wished she could paint with the painting itself in front of her, but that, of course, would be impossible.

"You have to be good enough, Calli," she could hear Arie telling her once more. "I know you are — prove it to me."

"I will, Arie," she breathed. "I will."

Having completed as much as she possibly could in one night, Calli gathered her sketchbook under her arm and quietly let herself out of the study as she began to sneak back down the corridor. She had to admit that she didn't overly enjoy such subterfuge, which made her question whether or not she was fully one of her family.

None of them seemed to be concerned on the ethics of what they did — not even Xander, who was as close to her as any other person could be.

She was so wrapped up in her thoughts that she wasn't paying attention to any of the sounds the house revealed to her, and when she turned the corner, she ran right into a very solid figure.

"Oh, bollocks!" she cried, stumbling backward as her sketchpad fell out of her hand and tumbled to the floor, although she retained her hold on the candle, luckily not allowing the small nub of remaining tallow to light anything on fire.

"Miss Donahue!" the duke said as he held out a hand to steady her, and she jumped when his warm, strong fingers brushed against her elbow. She wished he wouldn't call her Miss Donahue. It wasn't her name, and she realized with some shock she would love to hear her own upon his lips, not the name of another. But of course, he would never know her as Calliope Murphy. For if he did, then he would most certainly be sending her out of his house, her arse to the street.

"Are you all right?" he asked, his low voice nearly a caress, and she nodded hastily.

"Just fine. I am so sorry, Your Grace."

They crouched at the same time to pick up her sketchbook, and even while wincing as they bumped their heads into one another's, Calli managed to sneak out a hand and grab her incriminating work before the duke had a chance to see it.

"I'm sorry again," she said, biting her lip as she rubbed her forehead. "That was very poorly done of me."

"Nothing to be sorry for," he said, reaching up a hand to

brush her curls away from her forehead as he narrowed his eyes to inspect it. "Have I caused any damage?"

"No," she said, her eyes fluttering at the softness of his touch upon her skin. What was wrong with her? She was acting like no man had ever come close to her before. "I shall be fine."

He ignored her, stepping closer to further satisfy himself.

"I've been told I have a hard head," he said, one corner of his lips tilting — ever so slightly, but tilting — upward.

"Was that... was that a joke, Your Grace?" Calli asked, her eyes widening, and at her startled stare, he let out a bark of laughter.

"I suppose it was. Is that so terrifying a thought?"

"No, I just never... I thought that... well, I am surprised is all," she managed, even as she knew she was likely digging herself deeper into trouble.

"The idea isn't strange to me," he said softly, his voice faraway, as though he had forgotten she was even there. "It's just a bit more... absent than it once was."

"Why is that?" she asked, even as she knew she shouldn't. It wasn't her place, and he certainly didn't seem like a man who was going to share any part of himself, most especially not with his governess.

"Life has a way of making one a bit more cynical. Less trustworthy," he said, his face closing off, his smile completely vanished, and Calli wished she could take back the question to welcome forth the laughing, smiling man once more. "Speaking of trust, what are you doing wandering around my house in the middle of the night?"

"Is it?" she squeaked. "The middle of the night, that is? I hadn't realized. I was..." well, she supposed she had to tell the truth of it now, or her lie would be obvious. "I was sketching."

"Sketching."

"Yes."

"And just what, Miss Donahue, do you sketch?"

He was too close now, and Calli found her breath flowed quite rapidly even as she wished that he wasn't the man he was, this intimidating duke who she was currently practically relying on to survive.

"Everything," she said, telling the truth. "People, landscapes, objects… I like to sketch a variety of subjects."

"I see. And why are you sketching here in the corridor, in the middle of the night?"

"I was sketching the moon," she said, hoping that he wouldn't ask to see her work. "I had a hard time seeing it from my window." Was that even true? She wondered, trying to determine the direction of the house and just where the moon would be in relation to it.

He seemed satisfied enough with her answer, however, for he stepped out of the way and allowed her passage by him. "I hope it was worth it, Miss Donahue," he said. "It can become rather chilly down here at night."

"I have realized that now, Your Grace," she said as she stepped around him, relieved and yet somehow not entirely eager to leave him. When she stared into his face, there was a sense of… loneliness, sadness even, overwhelming him. When she peered closer, however, he seemed to sense her scrutiny and jerked his shoulders back, tossing his head high as though ready to start a battle.

"Well. If you require anything, please ask Mrs. Blonsky or one of the maids," he said with a curt nod of his head, back to business once more.

"Of course," Calli murmured, even though she had quickly found out that as a governess, she was not respected by the housekeeper nor accepted by the maids. She was between worlds here, just as she was at home.

She knew she should take his offered passage, continue

down the corridor and up the stairs to find her room once more. No proper governess would linger here in the hall with her employer in the middle of the night, staring so intently at him, eager to learn and devour his secrets.

But then, Calli wasn't exactly a proper governess. And behind all of his stern words and standoffish gestures, Calli could sense that there was more to this duke than what he wanted everyone to think. And even though she was here for an entirely different purpose, even though she had no cause to spend any time with this man let alone speak to him about anything besides the children, she couldn't seem to keep herself away from him.

She shifted her sketchbook out of her hand into the crook of the elbow of the arm that was holding the candle, freeing up the fingers of her other hand, which seemed now to be acting of its own accord. It inched away from her, up, up, toward the duke, who stood impassively, too polite to bat her hand away and yet obviously horrified by the thought that she might touch him.

Like she would have for any of her siblings or a child, she drew her fingers over his forehead, trying to erase the crease in his brow, the lines of worry that seemed so deeply ingrained they would never leave him.

She waited for him to flinch, to pull away, but he surprised her when he closed his eyes and leaned into her touch.

"You carry many burdens, Your Grace," she said, her words just over a whisper.

He nodded slightly. "Most men of my status do."

"But you allow them to bury themselves deep within you, to cause such torment in your soul."

"I do not," he rebutted, and she smiled slightly at his refusal to allow her to lift the burden of them for even this one moment.

"You must release them," she said, trailing her fingers over his temple now, down his cheekbone, until she cupped his tense jaw. "Allow peace to flow instead."

Her brother had taught them all many years ago of the ancient practice of sitting silently, allowing their thoughts to rein freely and find peace. Calli had never seen a man more in need of it.

"I cannot," he said, his jaw still held stiffly. "For then, who would take them up?"

"They would still be there waiting for you," she said, "but everyone needs some solace now and again."

His eyes snapped open, finding hers, and he stepped toward her so suddenly that her arm fell at her side.

"Not everyone has time for running on the green and painting the moon, Miss Donahue," he said, his voice as harsh now as the planes of his face in the dim light. "Be sure to teach the children *that* as well."

And with that, he broke away, striding down the hall and into his study, returning to his work once again.

CHAPTER 6

The woman was some kind of witch.
That was the only explanation for the enchantment she had seemed to place over him last night as he had stood there with her cool, soothing fingers upon his face.

He never let anyone that close. Never.

Not physically, and certainly not emotionally.

No, Jonathan was just fine on his own, and he didn't need any capricious governess trying to absolve him of all of his problems.

Others had tried to come close to him before, and it had always ended in disaster. He wasn't about to allow it now.

Even if, in that one moment, it had felt so good to rest his head against her hand and allow her to soothe him.

But now, in the light of the next day, he had returned to sanity and the truth of his life. A dangerous life of lies.

Before business, however, he had promised Davenport to meet him for a morning ride. After mounting his horse, General, Jonathan had led him into a warm-up walk before finishing with a trot as they entered Hyde Park. Jonathan could admit that one of the aspects he did enjoy about being in the country, as far as it took him from all of his business interests, was the freedom of riding. It was the only place where, as his infernal governess put it, he could be free and release those burdens.

But for now, the park, which should hopefully be nearly empty this early in the morning, would have to do.

"Davenport," he greeted his waiting friend, who always looked as free as Jonathan did burdened. "Fine morning."

"It most certainly is," the marquess said. "You left the Sheffields early last night."

Jonathan shrugged. "I had other matters to attend to."

"You know, if you spent as much time charming young ladies as you did studying your ledger book, you would either be London's most notorious rake or a happily married man," Davenport said with a laugh, and Jonathan snorted as he shook his head.

"I don't have much care to fall in love, Davenport, you know that."

"But your mother expects you to marry. And she will be returning from Bath in the near future."

"Yes, and then she can look after those little hellions."

"I thought you found a governess."

"I have."

"Well, then, what does your mother's return matter?"

Jonathan sighed. "I was hoping the children would keep her distracted from her intentions to see me wed by the end of this season."

"Because she would far prefer that you had a wife who would be responsible for the children."

"That is not entirely true."

"But partly."

"Partly, yes, most assuredly," Jonathan said with a curt nod. "But for now, our current arrangement will have to do. Finding a wife has proven far too time-consuming."

"I don't know how you do it," Davenport said, shaking his head.

"Do what?"

"Spend so much time with your work, your investments. Where is the joy in that?"

It was curious that Jonathan and Davenport had become such fast friends, for they viewed life completely differently. Davenport was all about finding the fun that life had to offer, which seemed to work just fine for him. But whenever Jonathan tried to follow suit, he was left unsettled, unsatisfied.

And then there had been the one time when he had allowed his heart to open. Look where that had gotten him.

"You're thinking of her again," Davenport said, causing Jonathan to swerve his gaze back toward him.

"Who?"

"You know who. The person I know you're thinking of when your face closes off darkly."

"I do not think of her."

"No?" Davenport said, lifting one of those black brows in the expression that caused women to fall at his feet. "Is she not the reason you now are who you are?"

Jonathan grunted. "If anything, I should be thankful to her. For she taught me that I need to be careful who I trust, that I need to keep my guard firmly in place. Most people who I meet want something from me. She was no different, and I should have known better."

"She turned you into a cynical man," Davenport said, something close to regret lacing his voice. "Not everyone is out to get you."

"Most are. Or out to get *something*. She wanted my name, my wealth, a man who would never question her for fear he would lose the respect that meant so much. I am only glad I discovered the truth when I did."

"For that, I suppose, you can most certainly be grateful," Davenport said with an audible exhale. "Well, enough chatter for one morning. What do you say we race?"

"I say it's about time," Jonathan said, relief sweeping over him that Davenport had finally left the issue alone.

"The tree down there," Davenport said, pointing into the distance. "The one that was cracked in the storm, with the fallen branches. We'll race there."

"Are we wagering?"

Davenport's normal smile now widened into a huge grin.

"Of course. What would you like to wager?"

"If I win, you never discuss my past again," Jonathan said, hardness in his voice that caused Davenport to narrow his eyes at him.

"And if I win?"

"What do you want?"

"A night with that lovely creature under your employ?"

"What are you talking about?" Jonathan asked sharply, his gaze swinging to his friend.

"The one playing with the children on the green in front of your house yesterday. She caught the eye of many a passerby."

Jonathan gritted his teeth. He knew he should never have allowed such a thing. He should have listened to his instincts.

"You know I can never agree to that."

"Keeping her for yourself?"

"No!" he barked. "She's a member of my staff and therefore under my protection. From men such as me — and you."

"Most men wouldn't agree with you."

"That is of no consequence."

Davenport sighed. "Very well. Five pounds will do."

With that, they counted down together before urging their horses on, across the empty field toward the tree in question.

Jonathan's heart raced in time with his horse's hooves. Every gentleman loved to ride, it was true, but for him, riding was part of his very soul, the one time when his spirit soared free, when he felt like he was flying along with his horse. He could never properly explain it to anyone else, and when he had tried to broach the subject before, he had felt the fool, for no one seemed to properly understand the pure joy it brought him. But joy it did bring.

He became so caught up in floating over the air and the race against Davenport that he barely registered when the empty field was suddenly empty no longer.

A figure ran out in front of him, so small and slight that he nearly mistook it for an animal due to the speed of his own mount.

Jonathan cried out to Davenport even as he hauled on General's reins, as the horse gave a loud whinny of protest when he dug his back feet into the earth. Jonathan just managed to hold on and avoid flying over the horse's head as the child was suddenly covered from danger by the figure running after him, rolling over top of him and shielding him.

Even as the dust began to float down from the air surrounding them and settle to the ground, there was no mistaking who was before him.

His governess, the woman who, apparently, all of London was talking about if Davenport could be believed, was curled into a ball around his nephew.

* * *

CALLI SQUEEZED her eyes shut tight as she waited for the horse's hooves to pound over her, and she prayed that she could keep Matthew out of harm's way.

When the impending doom didn't arrive, she cracked open one eye and then the other, even as Matthew began to squirm in her arms, apparently no worse for his near brush with death.

"Miss Donahue," he grunted as he squirmed. "Miss Donahue!"

"Miss Donahue!" Another voice came from behind her, and she closed her eyes once more when she heard it. The intensity of it was enough to remind her that *she* was Miss Donahue. At least for the time being.

That voice did not sound particularly pleased so she decided to just ignore it for a moment.

She released Matthew, setting him back on his feet.

"Are you all right?" she asked, running her hands over him. "Are you hurt at all?"

"No," he said, shaking his head. "I'm fine."

"Oh, Matthew, you had me so worried," she said, her heart still pounding in her chest. She could still see him running out in front of the horses, sure that he was going to be trampled to death. She would never have been able to bear it.

Mary came running up to them and immediately began to scold her brother. "That was stupid," she said, her hands on her hips. "You were nearly killed."

"I was not!"

"You were too!"

"Everyone is fine," Calli said as she turned over, except that as she did, she realized there was one person who was not entirely fine.

"Matthew, Mary!"

They all turned as one to see the duke striding toward them, his gait powerful, purposeful, and altogether displeased.

"Your Grace," Calli said, attempting to get to her feet to curtsy, but as she stood, she nearly fell back over when her ankle didn't seem to want to cooperate and hold her up.

"What is the meaning of this?" the duke thundered, and

Calli winced as she placed a hand on the shoulders of Matthew and Mary, in part to offer them her support and in equal part to hold herself up.

"I'm sorry, Your Grace," she said, still slightly winded from her sprint across the park. "Matthew got away from me and by the time I caught up, I was nearly too late."

When the duke lifted his hat and wiped a hand across his forehead, Calli realized that he was not so much angry, but he was *worried* — which, she supposed, was a stride in the right direction to actually caring for the children.

"My God, Matthew, you were nearly killed — by my own horse," he said, horror in his voice at the thought of just what could have happened.

"Luckily you appear to be a rider of great skill," Calli said in an attempt to lessen the severity of the duke's anger. "You managed to stop in good time."

"Yes," he said, turning his stormy gaze toward her, "but if you hadn't caught Matthew, it would have been Davenport who would have run over the child."

"Although I like to think that I am of equal, if not greater skill to Hargreave here," said a handsome man with light, curly locks escaping from beneath his hat as he strode over from where the horses were now tied, sending Calli a wink and then a grin that she couldn't help but return. He was an attractive man, that was for certain, and obviously a charming one as well. Was he really friends with the duke?

Calli's employer turned his withering stare on the man and shook his head.

"Not right now, Davenport," he said before looking at Calli, his gaze now levelled, something in his eyes akin to... was that respect? "You risked your life for my nephew, Miss Donahue."

Calli shook her head, not wanting such praise. She didn't

deserve it. "I was just trying to keep him safe, Your Grace. Anyone would have done the same."

"They most certainly would not have," he said, his voice brokering no argument. "Assuredly none of the boy's other governesses. Now, I'm also not sure that any of them would have had the courage to take these two children into Hyde Park, but as you were foolish enough to do so, I appreciate what you were willing to do."

She nodded. "Thank you, Your Grace," she said, unsure how else to respond to what she assumed was a compliment, coming from him.

"Since you are here, now, Uncle, would you like to spend some time with us?" Matthew asked eagerly, sweeping his arm back behind him. "Miss Donahue said you couldn't accompany us because you are working, but it seems that you are riding."

"That was yesterday," Calli murmured toward him, her cheeks burning hot at being caught in the lie, even by a child. "Your uncle is a busy man." She turned back to the two gentlemen. "We shall be going. Come along, children."

She began to urge them back toward the path, but as she tried to step onto her right ankle, she gave a hiss of pain.

"Miss Donahue?" the duke stepped toward her. "Are you all right?"

"Just fine," she said, waving him away, wishing he would leave now. She was sure if she was able to make it back to the carriage and the footman who awaited them, they could be home quickly, before she made a spectacle of herself.

"It looks to me that you have injured your ankle."

"It's just a sprain, I'm sure of it," she insisted, knowing that it would hurt a great deal more if it were anything worse. She had experienced such injuries before.

"Sit."

"Oh, no, really, I—"

"Sit."

When the Duke of Hargreave commanded someone, it was obvious that he accepted no answer but acquiescence. Even the children looked at her with the expectation that she obey. Calli sighed and sat down on the grass, even as the second gentleman crossed his arms over his chest and looked on with a smug grin on his face that Calli didn't quite understand.

The duke held out his hands to her, and she looked up at him, confused. From what her siblings had told her, gentlemen were not supposed to touch ladies in public. Except, she supposed, she was not exactly a lady and they were not exactly in public.

"No need to be afraid of me ravishing you in the middle of Hyde Park," he said rather snidely, earning snickers from Matthew and Mary — and his friend, who at least tried to cover his with a cough.

"I would never dream of such an occurrence, Your Grace," she said, holding her head high, knowing that he would never deign to consider a dalliance of any sort with a woman like her — a woman in his employ, far from the standard of delicate beauty he would be used to.

She did, however, remember Diana's suggestion that Calli would make a most enticing mistress for a gentleman, should the situation ever require it. Arie had become so angry at the idea of it, however, that Diana had quickly abandoned it.

When Calli found herself nearly trembling at the duke's strong, firm fingers near her ankle, however, she pushed the thought away as quickly as it had invaded.

He didn't look at her as he deftly untied the laces of her boot before slowly sliding it down her foot. It would have been a seductive moment in itself had it not caused a bolt of pain to shoot through her ankle, and she bit her lip to keep from crying out.

The duke's firm fingers now stroked over the stockings covering her leg, feeling for any damage, and he asked her to turn her foot one way and then the other, still not looking her in the eye.

"How does that feel?" he asked, finally looking up to meet her gaze, and she had to swallow hard when he did, for his eyes had turned a rather dark, intense shade of blue.

"I-it hurts a bit," she said, "but I can certainly still move it."

"Good," he said curtly. "Where's the carriage?"

"We left it — with the driver and the footman — near Rotten Row," she said.

"The footman should have accompanied you," he muttered, before turning his head, not letting go of her foot. "Davenport, would you make yourself useful and ride over to find the carriage? Tell the driver to bring it back here, closer to where we are. That way we won't be on display before the eyes of anyone out for an early stroll."

"I am not your servant, Hargreave."

The duke closed his eyes for a moment, clearly vexed.

"Please?" he said, the word nearly indecipherable due to the growl that accompanied it.

Davenport grinned in return. "Very well. Since you asked so nicely."

He began whistling as he strode back to his horse, and soon enough he was thundering by them, leaving the four of them alone.

"We'll meet them at the road," he said before lifting Calli's boot and attempting to slide it back on, but it was no use. The ankle was too swollen. "Damn it, I should have left the boot on," he said, lifting his hat and running his hand through his hair. "I cannot have you walking in your stocking feet. If you even are able to walk, that is."

"I am perfectly fine, Your Grace," she said, shaking her

head insistently. "Perhaps if the children can find me a stick of some sort, that would help me walk to the road."

She looked up at them with an earnest smile, but before anyone could respond, the duke had risen to his feet, and then was bending down, scooping his arms beneath her.

"Your Grace, what are you—" Calli exclaimed, but it was too late. She was in the duke's arms. And it didn't seem likely that he was letting her go.

CHAPTER 7

This was madness. All of it.

The ride through Hyde Park. The children's inability to behave. And this damned woman, who kept appearing everywhere he didn't want her to be.

Jonathan didn't know what was wrong with her — or with *him* — but it seemed she had somehow invaded his every sense. When he walked into a room, he sniffed for honeysuckle, when he took his breakfast, he listened for her sultry voice, when he strode down any London street, he looked for her shining head of black hair, even when he knew full well that she was at home under his own roof.

By God, he had only known her for two days, and she was his *governess*.

But who in their right mind would ever suggest this woman for a governess? Her lush curves sank into his arms as he carried her, his face far too close to her ample bosom, though it was tactfully covered. Now the scent he always searched for was not only present but somehow within him and he wondered whether he would ever be able to rid his nose of the honeysuckle that currently filled it.

"Matthew, Mary!" she called out, startling him.

He turned around to find the children were still waiting in the field. They answered her summons, running after them, apparently deciding to race one another.

"They really do need to learn to listen," she said, a frown on her face.

He grunted in response.

It was not that he was overly exerted from carrying her. It was that he was overly exerted from trying to keep command over all of the desires that were currently telling him to dump her into the carriage, climb in after her, and then shut the door to everyone else.

But, of course, there were the children. And Davenport. And her position in his household. And propriety. And everything else that would make that the entirely wrong thing to do.

Davenport beat the carriage back and seemed to accurately assess the situation in front of him.

"The carriage should be here in just a couple of minutes," he said, looking at Calli and then back at Jonathan. "Would you like me to hold onto Miss Donahue while we wait for it?"

His eyes sparkled, and Jonathan shot him a look that told him just exactly what he thought of his little jest.

"I am just fine."

"I can stand, really," Miss Donahue said from within the circle of his arms, but he ignored her. He *was* fine. Even if it was to himself that he needed to prove it.

"Does she need to see the physician, Uncle?" Mary asked.

Before he could say anything, Miss Donahue interrupted. "No, of course not. I'm sure I will heal in just a couple of days."

Jonathan looked down at her now, chagrined to find that

their faces were but inches away from one another, those plush red lips all too tempting.

"You could have been killed, you know," he said, his voice harsh. "*I* could have killed you."

"Enough of that," she scolded as if he was one of her charges. "No one was killed, and everyone is fine."

"Perhaps," he muttered. "But you shouldn't have taken such a risk."

"Of course I should have," she said indignantly. "I would never put a child's life before mine."

She looked past him, then, at the children, and he was struck by the honesty of her words. What kind of woman was she, that she would put the welfare of children she hardly knew before her own?

The carriage arrived before he could put voice to his thoughts, however, and he deposited her within it with as much gentleness as he could manage.

"I will meet you at home," he told both her and the children, bending to lift the two young ones into the carriage, not even realizing how naturally it felt to do so until after he had done it and the three of them were all watching him in awe.

He cleared his throat, hoping they wouldn't make anything of it, before he shut the carriage door, stepped back, and motioned the driver away.

Davenport was waiting.

"Say nothing," Jonathan growled.

"I—"

Jonathan shook his head and glared. "Not a word."

"Very well," Davenport said, taking the lead of his horse as they walked back to Jonathan's. But then Davenport began to whistle a tune that had Jonathan shaking his head as he hid the smile that threatened.

Lavender's Blue.

***

CALLI FOUND herself quite spoiled over the next day or two. The duke had arrived home and quickly checked upon her, asking her and Mrs. Blonsky whether a physician was required. When they answered in the negative, he continued on his way. Calli did her utmost to entertain the children from a sitting position, and even found herself attempting to teach some basic arithmetic.

She was only glad that her pupils didn't seem to be aware that she was not the most conventional of governesses.

Most of what she knew had been taught to her by Arie and then Diana, both of whom were more concerned about adding together figures in order to determine the worth of an item, how much expenses would cost them, and how to disperse their... earnings.

She tried to use much more appropriate items when teaching the children.

Apples, loaves of bread, bolts of cloth and the like. They were bright children, but bored easily, and Calli found herself grasping for ideas to entertain them.

"Let's play a game," Mary said decidedly one afternoon.

"Very well," Calli said, ready to accept any suggestion. "What were you thinking?"

"Hide and seek."

Calli mulled over the idea. Her ankle was healing, but she still found herself hobbling around.

"Only if we all stay on this floor," she said. "I cannot be hobbling up and down stairs at the moment."

"Of course," Mary said brightly, and when Calli eyed her suspiciously, the girl smiled brilliantly.

"You must listen to what I say, Mary," she tried to warn sternly.

"We always do," Matthew added unhelpfully, for they most assuredly always did *not*.

"You count first," Mary commanded, and Calli kept her eyes open a crack as she began. She wasn't surprised to see the children dart off and take for the stairs. Interestingly, they went up instead of down, and she smiled to herself before opening her eyes and pulling out her sketchpad.

Which was how the duke found her ten minutes later.

"Miss Donahue?"

"Your Grace!"

She shot up straight, her sketchbook falling onto the chair behind her as she struggled to her feet.

He looked around the room, his brow furrowed. "Where are the children?"

"We finished our arithmetic lesson, so as a reward we are playing a game. Hide and seek."

"I take it they are hiding?"

"They are."

"But you are not seeking."

Calli bit her lip and tried not to stare right into those eyes, which seemed to render her senseless.

"I told them to stay on this floor, but they disobeyed and went upstairs. There is nothing above us but some store rooms. They will quickly tire and realize that they have nothing to gain from continuing to hide."

"Until they continue up and reach the servants' quarters."

Calli's mouth gaped open. She hadn't considered they would go that far.

"I'll be right back," she said, limping out of the room as fast as she could, humiliation trailing after her. This man had a knack for seeing her at her worst. She held fast to the railing as she began to take quick, slightly painful steps upwards, until a large presence appeared beside her and lifted her lower arm onto his elbow.

"Allow me," he said taking her weight and half-lifting her up the stairs. She wanted to tell him she was just fine, that she didn't need his help, but they were both well aware how much of a lie that would be.

They reached the top level without incident, finding the rooms above empty of anything but old furniture and items for storage.

"Not here," Calli murmured, before there was a slight shriek from the very end, and then the giggles of two children as they raced into the room and began their sprint toward the staircase.

Which they stopped short of when they saw Calli and their uncle.

"Uncle. Miss Donahue," they both managed as they stared up at them, and Calli tried to hide her smile at the way they were trying to inch around the pair of them to the other side.

"Just what were you doing in there?" their uncle asked, raising a brow.

"Nothing!" Mary exclaimed at the same time Matthew said "hiding," in a bored tone.

"And now you have come out of your hiding place, have you?" Calli asked, placing her hands on her hips. "I told you to stay on the second floor."

"We tried," Mary said with a sigh, "but we were bored so we came up here. But then we found it boring here too."

"Until we found a spider," Matthew said with a grin, "so we put it in on one of the maid's pillows. Then we were coming back to you, Miss Donahue."

Calli rubbed the bridge of her nose, wondering how she was ever going to get through to these children.

"At least it wasn't your bed, Miss Donahue!" Matthew exclaimed at her look of chagrin. "We like you too much."

He seemed as pleased with the words as Calli was, but

now wasn't the time for praise. She awkwardly bent to kneel on the floor.

"That doesn't make it right, Matthew," she said. "Now that lovely maid will likely be unable to sleep."

He looked off in the distance, his actions and his conscience apparently at odds. "Very well," he muttered.

"Very well, what?"

"I won't do it again."

"Good. Now, back down to the nursery for you two. I've got a spider to catch."

The duke persisted in seeing her up the one flight of steps, where he left her, although Calli could feel every imprint of his gaze upon her back.

"Miss Donahue?"

She turned.

"You did well." He nodded, and then was gone, his enigma maintained.

* * *

Jonathan couldn't help the chuckle that escaped, fortunately long enough after Miss Donahue and the children were out of earshot.

She was surprising, this one. She most certainly was far from what he would ever expect from a governess in every way, but perhaps she was what these children needed.

He only wished that he wasn't so in tune with the sway of her hips as she walked away, nor quite so affected by the curl of her smile, the teasing look in her eyes as she regarded him, as though she knew exactly what he was thinking. He could only pray that she had no inkling whatsoever of his thoughts, for then he would be a doomed man.

"Your Grace?"

He turned to find his butler at the end of the hall,

watching him with an amused expression on his face that Jonathan had no wish to speculate about.

"Yes?"

"Shepherd is here to meet with you."

"Ah, good." How had he forgotten that his man-of-business was to arrive at this hour?

Oh, yes. Because Miss Donahue had distracted him.

Not on purpose, but still, distract him she had.

"Please see him into the study," Jonathan said, then turned around, clasped his arms behind his back, and returned to where he belonged.

CHAPTER 8

Calli stared at the note in her hands.
Family meeting. Xander will fetch you at midnight.
She sighed. There had been no mistaking that thick black scrawl. Arie expected her and she knew he would not take no for an answer. Even if her "no" was on account of her requiring more time to work on the painting.

The truth was, however, that while she was falling behind in her self-imposed timeline, she knew part of the reason she was doing so was her own self-doubt.

Not doubt in her abilities — she knew she was capable of replicating even a master, for it came down to copying, stroke for stroke. A true expert would realize that it was a fake, that was certain, but she wondered if the duke even appreciated what he had.

At least she tried to use that thought to make her feel better.

She balled the note in her hand now as she crept down the stairs and then through the house to the servants' entrance. Fortunately, all were abed now, the maids and the cook having to wake in just a few hours to prepare the household.

Calli herself would be getting no sleep tonight. She sighed once more dramatically as she let herself out into the cool night air, wondering how she was going to get through an entire day with two children and no sleep.

Obviously, her eldest brother didn't care.

"Calli!" Xander jumped out of the shadows, wrapping a hand around her arm so quickly that she jumped and would have yelped had she not been accustomed to expect the unexpected.

"Xander," she said, swatting him instead, "you nearly scared me half to death."

"Sorry," he muttered. "Best go quickly. Carriage is waiting."

Calli's family was one of the few living in St. Giles who could afford a carriage. But that was part of the spoils of their business — and also a necessary piece to many of their plots.

"What's wrong with you?" Xander asked, stopping suddenly, staring down at her ankle, and Calli realized belatedly that, while her ankle had healed quite a bit since her fall a few days ago, she was still favoring it.

"I rolled my ankle," she said, tugging at his arm and urging him forward, eager to have this meeting over and done with. If she was lucky, she might be able to return home for an hour or two of sleep.

Her breath caught.

Home? By home did she mean the duke's townhouse? She was obviously far too tired already for her thoughts weren't even making sense.

"How did you do that?" Xander asked, his brows furrowing together in concern.

"I had the children in the park," she said, deciding not to

elaborate any further. Xander had spent his life worrying about her, and there was no point in exaggerating that worry when there was really nothing to be done about it anyway.

"And?"

"And I had to chase one of them and rolled my ankle. It's fine. Nothing to concern yourself with."

He nodded as he held out a hand to help her up into the carriage, but when he turned and the moonlight struck his face, she saw the worry there and knew she was going to hear about it in his own Xander way.

"Calli, I'm worried," he said predictably as the carriage began trundling down the pavement, away from this expanse the duke — and apparently, now Calli — called home.

"Why?" she asked, turning her gaze on him, burrowing into her cloak for warmth.

"I don't like you all alone in that house, doing this without any support from the rest of us."

"I understand, but it's too late for that now, Xander. I can do this. You know I can. Arie has never trusted me with anything like this before, and I want to prove to him that I'm as worthy as the rest of you."

"Calli…"

"It's true. You have the quick hands, Diana has always been the manipulator, Damian has the brute strength, and Arie, of course, is the master schemer. I have barely done anything to earn my keep."

"That isn't true, and no one sees it like that. You help hold the entire family together."

"Well, maybe I want more."

The words were harsher than she meant them to be, and as Xander flinched and sank back into the shadows, she instantly wanted to recall them. But there was too much truth within them.

"We'll speak with the rest of them," he finally said,

crossing his arms over his chest and settling back against the squabs. Agreeing to disagree in silence, Calli closed her eyes for the rest of the short drive to St. Giles.

Which was why it seemed like just a few minutes later that she was seated in her usual place in the corner of the sofa, back within the comforts of her family home, in the company of those she loved more than any others.

It was a familiar scene, one that should fill her with warmth and the reminder of everything and everyone she loved.

But tonight she was uneasy, on edge.

"Calli," Arie said from his Louis XV chair with its off-white hide near the fireplace, looking his part of the head of a criminal organization. Even if that criminal organization was his family — a family that he had pieced together over the years. "It is good to have you home."

"It is good to be home, to see you all," she said, even as Damian nudged her playfully and Diana studied her thoughtfully. Nothing here had changed, it seemed. Diana was still suspicious of everything and everyone, including her own family.

"Diana told us all what happened the night of the party," Arie continued, his voice deep and unyielding, somewhat questioning. "You thought quickly on your feet."

"Thank you, Arie," Calli said softly, proud at his words.

"Are you sure, however, that this is a good idea?" Arie continued. "How is the work coming along?"

"The painting?"

"Yes."

"It is... coming. But slowly," Calli said, looking around, slightly uneasy to find them all staring at her with such question, as though they were wondering if this was something she could actually achieve. Well, she would show them all that they had not made a mistake in placing their faith in her.

"The painting itself hangs in the study, which makes it difficult to properly copy. However, I have the initial sketch completed and I hope to start painting tomorrow."

"Why is it taking so long?" Arie asked, ignoring the work she had already completed. Arie was never one to focus on accomplishments, always looking forward at what was still to come.

"I am with the children all day," she explained as best she could, hoping they would understand. "I hardly have a minute alone. It is not until everyone is abed that I can truly work, and even then, it isn't long as I have to rise early to see to the children's needs."

"How long until you are finished?"

Calli nibbled her lip as she considered the question. "Another two weeks, maybe three at most? It is an intricate painting with much detail."

Arie was silent for a moment, considering.

"Very well. Xander will continue to check up on you. In two weeks, we will plan a date to help you to switch out the paintings."

"Thank you," Calli said, glad that this had gone better than she had hoped.

"There's one other thing that Arie and I have discussed," Diana said, no longer silently watching, and Calli's heart dropped. She loved Diana, but Diana was rather... detached. Unsentimental.

"Yes?"

"Don't get close to those children, do you hear me?" she said, holding up a finger, although her face was not unkind. "You have a tender heart, Calli, and if you get too close to that family, you are likely to back out of this altogether. I know you."

"Calli?" Arie sat forward, peering into her face. "She's right."

"You have nothing to worry about," Calli said, leaning back self-righteously, annoyed that they would all doubt her, even though they had a point, for she was already feeling her fair share of pricks of guilt. "I am going to do this — to make you proud, to steal the painting, to help sell it for a great profit. It will turn out — just you wait and see."

* * *

JONATHAN RAN his hands through his hair as he paced the study back and forth.

Shepherd had presented him with quite the opportunity today. The question was, did he take the risk and go ahead, or stay the course?

If he bought the land attached to his current home in Kent, it could further his rents and estate for years to come.

But he had already decided to expand into shipping, and he didn't want to leave himself stretched too thin.

He was so caught up in his thoughts that he almost didn't hear the sound of a door closing, somewhere deep within the house. Almost.

But it was far too late for any servant to be up. He had even sent his valet to bed, telling him that he could manage, despite the servant's protest to the contrary.

He was going to leave the noise, sure that it was nothing of note, but then he worried that perhaps one of the children had risen from bed and was now wandering the house. Did children sleepwalk? Having little experience with children, he had no idea, but knew that a staircase could be treacherous for a young child who didn't know the house well.

He opened the door and walked to the foot of the stairs, looking up to see if anyone was about, but it was far too dark without any lanterns. He turned around to fetch a candle from his office — and ran right into a cloaked governess.

"Not again," Miss Donahue mumbled, and Jonathan nearly smiled, but he was too concerned as to where she had been and what she had been up to.

"Miss Donahue," he said dryly. "Fancy meeting you here in the middle of the night."

"You are awake quite late, Your Grace!" she exclaimed. "It's near four o'clock in the morning."

"Is it?" he said, aware that he should likely get to bed, but that was one of the most wondrous things about being a duke — he could sleep when he pleased.

Not that Jonathan slept much.

"So tell me, Miss Donahue," he said, ignoring her question, "just what are you doing up at such an hour?"

"I—" her mouth opened and closed as she seemed to be deciding what exactly she should say, and his eyes narrowed as he became aware that whatever she was about to tell him would be an obvious lie. "I had a family emergency arise."

"Oh?" he said, stepping back so that he could better assess the expression on her face. Unfortunately, the corridor was too dark to ascertain what she was thinking. "What kind of emergency would that be, requiring you to sneak out of your employer's house in the middle of the night?"

"I didn't want to go during the day and leave the children," she protested. "This seemed like the best time."

He didn't miss the fact that she was still avoiding his question.

"What was the emergency?"

"Does it matter?"

She held her chin up defiantly, and Jonathan wanted nothing more than to take that chin between his fingers and force her to realize that she was under his employ, that what happened to her mattered to him.

Although why, he couldn't have said for the life of him.

Her eyes glinted at him in challenge, however, and he

knew he would never win a battle with her by forcing her to reveal anything to him.

"If something is amiss… perhaps I can help," he offered, and she looked up at him with surprise.

"You could help?" she repeated incredulously.

"Of course," he said. "I consider anyone who works for me to be part of my family."

She snorted, causing him to take a step forward so he could try to ascertain just what she was thinking, throwing his words back in his face.

"You don't believe me?"

"You hardly consider your own niece and nephew as part of your family," she said, color rising to her cheeks as she likely realized she had said the wrong thing, although it didn't seem to stop her. "I hardly think you would feel such a thing about a woman you just met."

He was silent for a moment, anger brewing deep in his belly. Who did she think she was, this woman, to come into his house in the middle of the night and talk to him so?

"Miss Donahue—"

"Your Grace," she cut him off, holding up a hand, and he was too shocked to reply for a moment. "Please, before you say anything… my apologies. It's late. I'm tired, and I said things that I should not have said. Forgive me?"

She looked up at him in such supplication, he found he had no choice but to agree.

He couldn't help himself. He stepped ever closer. So close, that when he did what he had been longing to do and brought his thumb beneath her chin, she had no choice but to follow his silent command and bend her head backward to look up at him.

"You're forgiven," he whispered, his mouth but an inch away from hers, and he grinned in satisfaction when he caught the hitch in her breath. "But don't let it happen again."

Before he did something he knew he would forever regret, he released her abruptly and strode away.

It was only after she had escaped back up the stairs that he realized she never did tell him where she had been.

She had won, after all.

CHAPTER 9

Calli stilled herself mid-yawn when she sensed a presence in the room. For she knew without turning around exactly who it would be.

"Uncle!" Mary exclaimed, and Callie sighed before standing.

"Children," he greeted them perfunctorily before turning to Calli. "Miss Donahue. Tired, are we?"

"I'm perfectly fine," she said, even though she was perfectly longing to return to her bed and settle in for another few hours. Damn Arie and his late-night meetings. "What brings you here to the nursery, Your Grace?"

"Schoolroom," Matthew noted from the table in front of her.

She nodded. "Apologies, Matthew. The schoolroom."

"I believe I am allowed to go wherever I please in my own home, am I not?" he asked, and Calli's ears burned. It seemed she was forever saying exactly what she shouldn't. Would she ever learn proper manners before it was time to leave?

"I only meant... I was wondering if we could help you with anything."

"At ease, Miss Donahue. I was only teasing."

Calli's eyes widened as she stared at him. The Duke of Hargreave… teasing? She squinted as she studied him. Could that possibly be the hint of a smile dancing around his lips?

"As it is, I have some news for all of you. We are going to be travelling to the Kent estate for a short time."

Calli's heart began to beat loudly in her ears. To Kent? But what about her painting? How easy would it be to pack the canvas and her supplies and transport them there? How would her brother keep watch on her? This was not part of the plan. Not at all.

But it wasn't as though she was exactly in a place to voice those reservations.

"Is it not currently the Season, Your Grace?"

"It is, but we are coming close to the end and I'm sure Parliament will be fine without me for a short time. Let someone else worry about everything for a few days. I need to look at some adjoining land."

"The children and I could remain in London," Calli offered, her mind already speeding ahead, considering the ample amount of time she would have to sit and paint in the study, right in front of the original, without fear of being caught. Her memory was exemplary, that was for certain, and she had already managed a small reproduction to work from, but there would be no greater opportunity than painting with the work right in front of her.

"I'm sure it would be good for the children to get out into the country. Unless that is a problem for you, Miss Donahue?"

Calli forced herself to shake her head.

"No, most certainly not."

"Good. Be ready to leave by tomorrow."

"Tomorrow?"

Her head snapped up. She would have to work quickly to get word to her family.

"Yes, tomorrow," the duke said, his blue eyes staring near through her. "Is that acceptable to you, Miss Donahue?"

Noting his mocking tone, she nodded, although she didn't break his gaze, accepting the silent challenge he put forth to her before she returned her attention to the children, who wore grins now as they stared at their uncle.

"Grandmother isn't going to be there, is she?" Matthew asked with some trepidation, but Jonathan seemed to be covering a smile as he shook his head.

"We haven't been to Kent in some time, Uncle!" Mary exclaimed, to which the duke grunted.

"No. Business has kept me in London. But we should try to spend the summer there."

Mary and Matthew clapped their hands excitedly, and Calli couldn't help but look at them with a sad smile. She would be long gone from their lives by summer… another person who came into their world and then left, other priorities much more important.

But what was she supposed to do?

"Well, children," she said, brightly — perhaps too brightly, "I suppose that is enough spelling for today then. Shall we prepare for our journey?"

They agreed excitedly, beginning to run around the room and pack nearly every belonging they owned for the short stay.

As the duke walked away, his footsteps echoing in the near-empty corridor, Calli searched desperately for a piece of paper. She had a letter to write.

* * *

THE ART OF STEALING A DUKE'S HEART

JONATHAN PACED THE FOYER, arms crossed as he waited. And waited.

He was not a man of patience.

"Thurston!"

"Yes, Your Grace?" The butler stopped abruptly from the path he had been treading while overseeing the travelling arrangements.

"Where are the children? They were supposed to have been prepared to leave near an hour ago."

"I shall go check, Your Grace," he said, but before he could start up the stairs, a loud clatter arose from above, and soon the children were racing one another down the steps, with Miss Donahue in their wake.

She wore a creamy white gown today that accentuated her olive skin, and while he knew he should be reprimanding the children for running in the house and potentially falling down the stairs, he couldn't take his eyes off her.

She was stunning. He knew the gown was nothing particularly elaborate and would have been frowned upon by any self-respecting woman of the *ton*, but it didn't matter.

Miss Donahue reminded him of a goddess come to life. Before he could stop himself, before he even knew what he was doing, he had stepped up to the stairs as though he was escorting her through some ball and held his arm up to her.

Her eyes flashed in surprise, but she placed her fingers upon his arm anyway, letting them rest tentatively.

"Your Grace?" her lips parted on the near breathless words.

"You're late."

Well, that was not exactly what he had meant to say, but it was the only thing that came to mind besides telling her just how beautiful she was, which he absolutely could never do.

The spell between them broken, she dipped her head. "My apologies. There was just so much the children wanted to take with them. We must have packed and re-packed dozens of times, but it should all be prepared now and in the carriage."

Her gaze flicked through the doors to the waiting carriage out front as though it held her most prized possessions, which was ridiculous of course. The woman would have nothing more than a few gowns and whatever materials she used for teaching the children.

"Very well. Off we go now. Children, into the carriage."

He led her out and held up a hand to help her in. She turned around, looking back over her shoulder, her hat dipping low over her eyes, and Jonathan had to stifle a groan at the picture she made, half-bent so that she wouldn't hit her head on the door.

"Are you not coming?" she asked, and Jonathan was tempted to run up the carriage steps and follow her in.

But that would never do.

He shook his head adamantly. "I shall ride General beside the carriage. We haven't far to go."

She nodded and disappeared, though Jonathan couldn't avert his gaze until his groom appeared with his horse.

"Your Grace."

"Thank you," he murmured.

And they were off, without a look backward.

* * *

CALLI PEERED OUT THE WINDOW, grateful that the duke hadn't turned around.

For if he had, he might have seen a tall presence lurking within his front rose bushes.

A presence who looked an awful lot like Calli herself.

Lifting the curtain of the window on the side opposite the duke, Calli stretched her hand out into the air with a quick wave for Xander. Her note had gotten through to her family. They knew where she would be and hopefully wouldn't worry about her. At least not too much.

She drew in a breath as she leaned back against the squabs. *She*, however, was worried. Worried about the effect the arrogant, belligerent duke was having on her. He was too handsome for his own good, and while Calli typically despised men who told her what to do, somehow when the duke commanded her, it sent delicious thrills down her spine.

And here she was, working on swindling him, stealing his most prized painting. She wondered if he would have more adorning the walls of his country home. Would there be a gallery of paintings, she wondered? And just what would she do if there was?

She groaned at her wickedness. She was caught between two worlds, and she had to admit that she didn't properly belong in either one. But her family was her family. Arie had taken Xander in for his abilities, and had agreed to look out for her as well. She was finally repaying him the only way she could, and she couldn't take that responsibility lightly.

"Miss Donahue? Are you all right?"

Calli cracked open an eye to peer across the carriage at the children, who were staring at her with a great deal of concern, and she managed a smile for them.

"Just fine. My apologies."

"You look like you swallowed a grasshopper," Matthew said, his face screwed up as he studied her.

She barked out a laugh at that. "And just how do you know what it looks like to swallow a grasshopper?"

"We tried it last summer."

"Oh," she said, not wanting to pursue *that* matter any further — although she did have to make sure they wouldn't do it again under her watch. "And… how did you find that?"

"Not something worth repeating."

"Oh, good," she said, exhaling slowly.

"Let's play a game," Mary said.

"Very well. What shall we play?"

At Mary's request, they began a game in which they had to guess objects through clues, and when Mary said she spied something black, Calli knew, following her gaze, that it was her uncle's jacket. As she guessed correctly, she couldn't keep herself from watching the duke. He was so proper, so particular, so focused on doing what he was supposed to do. She wondered if he knew what it was like to have fun, if he ever threw off the cloak of responsibility to discover what else life had to offer.

Then he turned toward the carriage, causing Calli to quickly drop the curtain as she slammed back into the seat.

But it was too late. He had seen her.

* * *

"Your Grace?"

Jonathan rode closer to the carriage and when Miss Donahue stuck her head out — this time wanting his notice. He had to say he had enjoyed seeing her flustered when he had caught her staring.

"Yes?"

"The children would like a break."

"We shall be there shortly."

"Yes, I know, but perhaps, if there is a chance, they could stop and stretch their legs? Cook packed a lunch as well. It might be nice to eat outdoors."

Jonathan looked at the road ahead with longing. He hated to delay travel, but he supposed with children, one must, now and again, make allowances.

"Very well," he grumbled, riding forward to speak with the carriage driver.

Soon they came across a small clearing on the side of the road, and they pulled over and alighted. The children bounced out of the carriage as though they had been trapped within for days instead of hours, Mary executing a perfect cartwheel as they ran across the clearing.

"Children!" Jonathan called after them, but Miss Donahue waved a hand. "They won't go far. They're too hungry."

She was right. Soon enough they came wandering back, eager to discover the contents of the basket Calli held within her hands.

Jonathan had to admit that he was equally curious.

Packed on top of the food was a blanket that Miss Donahue stretched out on the grass before she began to pull out chicken legs and various fruits and vegetables.

She looked up at him from beneath her lashes when his stomach growled.

"Perhaps you *were* hungry," she said teasingly, and he grunted in response, not willing to accede.

She was right, however, which must have been apparent when they all dove in and began to eat, so focused that they didn't say anything for a few minutes as they stared out ahead of them at the wide open fields and forest beyond.

"Is this what your land looks like?" Miss Donahue asked him, and he nodded. "Some of it. The parts that aren't currently used for agriculture."

"I see. I'm sure we would love a tour of it once we arrive."

"Perhaps," he said, not promising anything.

"Miss Donahue, Uncle, shall we play a game?" Matthew asked once he was done, and Jonathan waved him on.

"You go ahead."

"A quick game of tag, please?" he asked, looking at them pleadingly. "It's not much fun with just two."

"Very well," Miss Donahue said, "I shall play for just a few minutes, and then we must continue on. Your uncle has much work to do in Kent. Now, get running, for here I come!"

The children took off with shrieks while Miss Donahue followed with a laugh. Jonathan sat back, wrapping one arm around his knee as he watched them. What would it be like, to be so carefree, to be able to run without so many responsibilities weighing one down, near choking him?

He didn't have much longer to think about it, for Matthew ran by and slapped him on the shoulder.

"Uncle, you're it!"

"Pardon me?"

"You're it!" Matthew laughed as he ran away, and Jonathan slowly got to his feet, looking around to see where the rest of them were. Little Mary was near Matthew, while Miss Donahue, perhaps not realizing the threat he posed yet, was nearing him.

The color had risen in her cheeks from her exertions, her bonnet was hanging down her back from its ribbons, and her hair had escaped most of its pins, tangled around her head in a riot of wild black curls — curls that he longed to reach out and capture within his fingers.

"Miss Donahue!" he called out, and she turned to him, her chest heaving from running. "Here I come!"

She let out a yelp as he began to give chase, and he caught her just as she began to run down an incline. He tripped as he reached out toward her, and before he knew it he had lost his footing and was falling to the ground, taking her with him.

He managed to turn at the last moment, taking her weight so that she wouldn't be hurt, and the two of them tumbled over one another until they finally came to a rest.

Mortified, Jonathan pushed himself up and hovered

overtop of her. "Miss Donahue, are you injured? Did you hurt your ankle again? I'm so sorry, I—"

She looked up at him with bright, laughing eyes.

"Nothing to worry about. I am just fine."

"But—"

"I'm fine," she insisted, reaching her hand up to cup his cheek, and he couldn't help but lean into it, her touch soothing, calming. "Are you?"

"Yes," he said, nodding slowly. "Yes, I am."

He forgot everything in that moment. Everything but her, this woman in front of him. Below him. He leaned down slowly, seeing nothing but those plush red lips, wanting nothing other than to feel them on his.

"Miss Donahue—"

"Call me Calli," she whispered, and he blinked.

"Calli."

He leaned in, about to take her lips—

"Uncle!"

And sighed. He closed his eyes for a moment then met her amused gaze as he pushed himself to his feet while his niece and nephew came running to check on them.

He didn't know whether to be regretful or thankful for their presence.

For he had been about to do something he had no right in doing.

But something that he wanted to do very, very much.

CHAPTER 10

Calli did her utmost to carefully ignore the duke.

She could feel his gaze upon her as she re-entered the carriage, her heart still pounding from the game of chase — a game that had ended very differently than she ever could have expected.

He had nearly kissed her. There, in a field in the middle of nowhere, and in front of his niece and nephew, no less.

Calli brought a hand to her lips, wondering what it would have felt like had they not been interrupted. Would he have kissed as intensely and as purposefully as he seemed to do everything else? Would he have been cold and refined, or rough and demanding?

It was hard to know who he was deep within, as opposed to the façade that he presented to the world.

He had been correct that Wyndmere, his estate in Kent, was not particularly far from their luncheon location, and it was impossibly too soon that he was holding out a hand to help her down from the carriage. She had to will every ounce of courage she possessed to look him in the eye as he did so.

Much to the children's chagrin but to her delight, once

they were inside he soon took himself deep within — likely to his study, Calli supposed — and they were left alone with the housekeeper, who greeted them enthusiastically.

"Hello! You must be the governess. And you, Mary and Matthew, have grown considerably since I last saw you."

The children looked up wide-eyed at the plump, spirited housekeeper who beamed down at them as they tried to make out what she was saying through her thick Scottish accent.

"Thank you?" Mary said, scratching her head.

"Come now, let's take you up to your rooms and then you can be off exploring."

They followed her up the huge front stairway, which had even Calli looking around in wonder. The curving bannister with its mahogany handrail was polished near shining, and everywhere she looked it seemed there were portraits and landscapes staring down at her. Were these the work of masters or had they been commissioned for the family — perhaps both? She wished she was better educated, but from what she could tell they were all done with a hand that certainly possessed great talent.

She sighed, wishing she could remain and study the work at length, but when she looked up, it was to find that the children were already at the first landing. She hurried up after them, the paintings reminding her of her own and the importance of keeping it from any prying eyes. She had been so rattled from her encounter with Jonathan that she had forgotten to fetch her things herself, and was now looking around desperately for her bags.

"Mrs.…."

"McDonald."

"Mrs. McDonald, do you know where our bags might be?"

"I imagine one of the footmen will be delivering them to

your rooms around the time we get there," she said, looking back at her. "Is there anything you need? I'm sure we can come up with something."

"It's fine," Calli said, knowing that there would be no reason for any footman to go through her things. She took a breath at the children's quizzical expressions and followed them up, eager to continue on the tour.

The nursery was most certainly designed for young children, and when she pushed open the door, it creaked from disuse.

"Apologies," Mrs. McDonald said with a shrug. "There hasn't been much need for the room in many years. But we've cleared away the cribs and rockers, and moved in a couple of beds for the children. Miss…"

"Donahue."

She truly hated to use the name of another woman as her own, but it wasn't as though Calli had much choice.

"Your room is just across the hall. There's an adjoining sitting room as well."

"Thank you, Mrs. McDonald."

"Of course. Anything you need, just ask. Now, as much as I would love to stay with ye for the rest of the day, I best be going."

Calli smiled warmly at the woman who had been more welcoming than the rest of the staff thus far.

With relief, she saw a footman approach, carrying their bags, and she had to stop herself from running down the hall to take hers from him.

"Well," she said to the children with a smile, "what do you say we do a little exploring?"

They eagerly agreed, and they spent the rest of the day looking down corridors and finding hidden rooms, the children taking great delight in playing underneath sheets that had been draped over furniture in parlors and in bedrooms that hadn't seen guests in obviously quite some time. Calli, who had always been used to a house — a smaller house of course, but a house still — that was practically bursting with people, found it rather sad. Lonely. How long had the duke been by himself? Where was his mother? Did he have any other siblings besides Mary and Matthew's mother? Cousins? Or had he always been alone?

It would explain a lot if he didn't, Calli mused, as she followed the children down the hall, catching up to them when they stopped by what was apparently a locked door.

"It won't move!" Matthew grunted as he tried to open it. Calli attempted herself, wondering if it was just stuck, but it was most definitely locked.

"Hmm," she said. "I'm not sure what it could be."

"What could Uncle have hidden away?" Mary asked, her lips turning down as though her uncle had purposefully hidden something just from her.

Calli crouched beside her and squeezed her hand.

"I'm sure it's just because there is something unsafe in there. Or something valuable."

Valuable. Calli considered the make up of the house and where they were situated. She didn't know particularly much about large estates such as this one, but she would have guessed there would be a room like a large gallery up here. It was what she had been hoping for, anyway. Was Jonathan hiding more priceless paintings up here?

She bit her lip. She had no wish to steal anything further from him. And yet, if Arie ever found out and knew she had been here…

"We best get back to the nursery," Calli said, deciding she would think on it later, not having the heart to do so now. "It must be near dinner time."

"Do you think we can dine with Uncle?" Mary asked eagerly. "Maybe it's different here in the country."

Calli wasn't so sure.

"I don't know—" she began, but they had just reached the stairwell and found Mrs. McDonald bustling by. "His Grace asked me to share that dinner shall be at eight o'clock."

"For all of us?" Calli asked her as she continued on.

"For all of you!" Mrs. McDonald called over her shoulder with a smile, and Calli turned to find the children beaming up at her.

"Well, then," she said to Mary. "I suppose you were right after all."

Now she just had to get through dinner without throwing herself at the duke. Surely that shouldn't be a problem. Should it?

* * *

JONATHAN KNEW this had likely been a bad idea.

But there was something about this big empty house out here in Kent that made him lonely. Even lonelier than usual. He didn't want to admit it, but it was, in truth, the reason he spent most of his time in London. Kent held too many memories — happy and unhappy. Of his father, who had left him far too young. His mother, who's interest in his life was negligent at best. His sister, the only person he had left in the world, who had abandoned him with her two children.

Besides, what was he supposed to do with himself in this lofty home alone?

At the very least, he wouldn't have to entertain the children himself over dinner. For the truth was, he had no idea what to do with them, what to say to them. He cursed his sister anew, wishing he knew where she was so that he could tell her exactly what he thought of her decision to leave the children with him. She had said in her note that she hoped he would provide for them.

Of course he would provide for them. Of that, there was no question. He would have done so even had his sister not left.

He heard them down the corridor before he saw them, their footsteps pounding over the carpeted hardwood before Miss Donahue called after them to slow down and mind their manners. She stopped them before they reached the dining room, and he heard her remind them in hushed tones to be polite and mind their uncle.

He smiled to himself. Miss Donahue had been a rare find indeed… for more reasons than should matter.

Jonathan sighed. He was just going to have to wrest control of himself. He knew from the past that he couldn't fully trust just anyone — not even a governess who had come highly recommended.

He stood from the end of the table when they walked into the room.

"Uncle!" Mary exclaimed, even as Miss Donahue placed a hand on her shoulder in an attempt to curb her enthusiasm — although she wore a slight smile as well, and Jonathan could sense that she somehow approved of his invitation to them this evening.

"Mary. Matthew. Miss Donahue," he said, nodding to each of them in turn. "Shall we?" He swept his hand out to the table in front of him, and all three of them became rather wide-eyed at the elaborate settings.

"I've never seen so many spoons," Mary said, her voice just above a whisper as they took their seats, and Jonathan chuckled.

"Well, this will be the perfect opportunity for your

governess to school you in table manners, then, would it not?"

He looked over at Miss Donahue with a smile, surprised when what seemed like panic crossed her face, although she quickly covered it with a nod.

"Of course," she said as the footmen entered with the soup, placing a bowl down in front of each of them.

"How have you found Wyndmere?" he asked as he picked up the soup spoon, after which the rest of them followed suit.

"It is ginormous!" Matthew exclaimed, to which Miss Donahue let out a slight laugh.

"Gigantic or enormous, Matthew," she said softly, although not critically, before she turned the force of those violet eyes up at Jonathan, eyes that tonight matched the dress that she wore, as reserved as it was. Jonathan was no great expert in ladies fashion, but he had the impression that she was not the first owner of the dress — it did not seem to fit her properly and was worn in a few places. He had a sudden urge to see her in the finest silks and satins — silks and satins that he commissioned himself to drape her in. "You have a beautiful home, Your Grace," she said. "We are lucky to see it."

He shrugged self-consciously as Mary chimed in.

"We were exploring, and we found a locked room," she said, her voice just above a whisper as though she was sharing a great secret, her soup spoon clanging against the side of the bowl. "What have you hidden away, Uncle?"

"Mary," Miss Donahue admonished, but as her eyes flitted over him, he could tell that she was just as curious as the children were.

"Nothing," he said with a shake of his head. "A few valuables, is all, to be kept away so that they cannot be damaged."

"Is it art?" Miss Donahue asked, raising one eyebrow in

what he could tell she thought was a nonchalant manner. "You have a fine collection adorning the walls. I cannot imagine anything even grander."

Jonathan remembered the sketchpad he had found in her possession the one evening in London.

"Are you interested in art, Miss Donahue?"

The footmen cleared away the soup course and brought in the beef. Jonathan looked down the table, seeing the salad and cheese still in the center, and asked if Miss Donahue would pass it around.

"Of course," she said, her cheeks reddening. "And I would say that I appreciate beautiful paintings, but I know not much about them."

"Do you paint yourself?"

"As an idle pastime," she said, waving a hand in the air as though it was nothing. "My sketches and paintings are nothing exemplary."

"I should like to see them sometime."

"Oh, that would only embarrass me," she said, looking down at her plate, "for I'm sure you have seen the very finest."

"All art has something to offer, Miss Donahue," he said, looking at her curiously, now more interested than ever seeing her work. "It is why I find it difficult to answer the question of just who is the greatest master painter. For each has something to offer, and it is all a matter of taste."

"There is much truth in that," she agreed, but her attention wavered when the footmen appeared again.

"What is that?" Mary leaned in and whispered in her ear, though loud enough that Jonathan could hear.

"I'm sure it's quite tasty," Miss Donahue whispered in return, and Jonathan had to work hard to keep his laughter in check.

"I hope you enjoy the artichokes," he said with a nod, and Miss Donahue looked up in some relief.

"Of course, I know we will," she said, and their gazes held for a moment until Matthew caught her attention from the other side of the table.

"Which fork to do we use, Miss Donahue?"

"Which fork?" she repeated, before looking down at the array remaining. "Ah, I would say…" her gaze flickered over to Jonathan, seeing the smaller fork in his hand. "This one," she said holding it up.

"Miss Donahue," Jonathan said, suddenly curious and a slight bit suspicious about her lack of knowledge in one of the subjects every governess of noble children should be well versed in. Collins had highly recommended her, as had the additional references he had contacted. "Just where did you say you had your education?"

"Oh, I don't think I ever said," she said with a demure smile that wasn't fooling him.

"Then do tell," he said, waving out a hand in front of him as though clearing the air for her words.

"I wouldn't want to bore you."

"Bore away," he said, hearing the slight edge in his tone. He didn't enjoy it when people tried to evade him.

"Very well," she said, placing her utensils down in front of her, looking around the table at each of them. "Most of my education was taught to me by my brothers and sister."

"You have brothers and sisters?" Matthew asked eagerly.

"I do," she said with a small nod. "Three brothers and one sister."

"Lucky," Mary said, stretching out the word. "I would like a sister."

"You have me," Matthew said, crossing his arms over his chest with a frown.

Miss Donahue nodded. "That is right. You are fortunate to have your brother."

"Who is your family?" Jonathan asked, needing to know more.

"We do not have noble blood," she said quietly. "I hope that does not preclude me from this job?"

"I am not that conceited," he said indignantly, "as long as you provide the children with what they need to know."

"Of course," she said with a slight nod. "My family is in… trade."

"Trade."

"Yes."

"Interesting. I do a great deal of investments in shipping myself," he said.

"I didn't realize that many noblemen did."

"Most don't. They find it beneath them. But it makes me a good deal of money."

She nodded as the dessert course was brought in, much to the children's delight.

Miss Donahue laughed, a sound that Jonathan found he rather enjoyed.

"This is one course it doesn't look like we shall have to explain," she said with a grin toward him, and he shook his head.

"No, we do not."

She picked up one of the cakes to pass it to him.

"Would you like some?" she asked, and he shook his head, holding a hand up. He tried to keep himself from such enticements.

She shrugged and served herself enough for two. She dug in a spoon and at the taste of sugar on her lips, she closed her eyes and sighed, before licking off a spot of whipped cream that had remained on her plush upper lip.

Jonathan stilled, unable to remove his eyes from her.

She was sensual without trying to be, had stirred his curiosity for no grand reason other than she was different from anyone he had ever met.

Jonathan enjoyed certainty. He preferred to know what to expect, from himself and from others.

But at the moment, only one thing was certain.

He was in trouble.

CHAPTER 11

Calli thanked the duke, grateful that the dinner was over, as wondrous as the food had been.

The cook in London was excellent, of course, but Calli had never before experienced a feast as she'd just had. She had caught the duke staring at her after she had stuffed the dessert in her mouth, leaving her a slight bit ashamed over how gluttonous she must have appeared.

Between that and the fact that she clearly had no idea how to properly address such a meal, it was a wonder that he could even look at her, so obviously did adhering to such things appear important to him.

She settled the children into bed, a feat made difficult from their exuberance over the meal with their uncle and the sugar they had imbibed at the end of it.

Finally, mercifully, after insisting on more than one tall tale, they were sleeping, and Calli returned to her room, eager to spread out her canvas and get to work.

Only to find that she couldn't seem to sit still.

Perhaps she had eaten far too much sugar herself. Perhaps the duke's questions were nagging at her, unsettling her. Or perhaps she was too curious about just what was held in those secret rooms of his.

She opened her bag and found, at the bottom, the small kit that one of her siblings had packed for her. Only her family would consider a lock picking kit an essential item.

Calli opened the door, finding the corridor blessedly empty. She had no idea how much staff was employed here in the country home, but it seemed quite a small contingent for such a large house. The duke must not spend much time here.

She hurried up the stairs to the third floor, soon finding herself in front of the door. Her heart pounded, knowing she had no business being here, but finding herself overwhelmed with curiosity. It wasn't as though she was going to do anything with whatever she found, she told herself, even though she could practically hear Arie's voice in her head as she crouched in front of the door. She just wanted to have a look, to see what other masters could be lurking within.

She had never been the best lock picker. That had been one of Xander's specialties, which meant she didn't often have any reason to utilize such a skill. Arie had made them all practice, however, and Calli couldn't help but let out a small, triumphant, "yes!" of a whisper when she heard the lock click in the mechanism.

She stood and took the doorknob in her hand, but just as she turned it, she was suddenly snatched up from behind.

"Help!" she tried to cry out, even as a hand clamped over her mouth. She attempted to bite down on it, but strong arms held her firm.

"Miss Donahue," came a low, soft yet steely voice in her ear. "Looking for something?"

The arms loosened just enough to allow her to turn within them, and she found herself face to face with the duke. His expression was, well... slightly murderous.

"Your Grace," she managed. "How… unlikely to see you here."

"This is my home," he said through near-clenched teeth. "I believe I have the right to go where I'd like. As we have discussed before."

"Of course," she murmured, even as she wiggled in his embrace in an attempt to back away.

"And what," he bit out, "might you be doing?"

"I…" she tried to look around him, but he was too close, held her too tight. "I'm sorry, Your Grace," she near whispered. "I was just curious."

"I do hope that lock picking is not a skill that you plan on teaching the children."

"Of course not," she said, looking down at his chest, unable to meet his eyes anymore. "My sister often locked me out of our bedroom, so I learned as a child how to allow myself entry."

"I see," he said, his grip loosening slightly, although his eyes didn't lose their suspicion. "Well, Miss Donahue, you want to see what's within? Go ahead."

He released her so suddenly she nearly fell, and he gestured in front of him. As much as she would have liked to turn around and run for her room, Calli found that she most certainly could not back away now, and she took a hesitant step through the door.

Only to find Aladdin's cave awaiting.

* * *

JONATHAN KNEW that he should be irate at finding her here.

Snooping. Spying. Prying.

She had no business being here. In this room. In his home. In his life.

But he couldn't force her out of this house any more than

he could from the imaginings that wouldn't leave him. As soon as he'd found her, he should have sent her on her way, at least back to bed if not out of this house and his employ completely. And yet, instead, here he was, inviting her into his sanctuary.

"Oh, Your Grace," she said, a hitch in her voice. "This is… this is…"

He smirked at her loss of words. He hardly showed anyone this room. It hadn't always been locked. But with the children in residence, he had been worried that they would mistake the long gallery for a place they could run amok, and so had decided that it might be in his best interests to keep it locked.

It seemed there was someone else who found the room captivating.

"How did you come to discover your passion for art?" Jonathan asked quietly, watching the rapture on Miss Donahue's face as it danced over the paintings that adorned the tall walls from ceiling to floor.

She took a few steps into the room, her hand hovering overtop of one of the sculptures that stood atop a pillar. "May I?" she asked quietly, and at his nod, she ran her hand reverently over the top of the bald man's head.

Suddenly Jonathan had a sudden wish to be a statue.

"I suppose I first fell in love with the paintings I saw in my brother's collections, which he acquired for clients," she said as she began to wander around the room, taking a closer look at the paintings he had collected over the past ten years. "I asked for paints, and soon found myself nearly obsessed with it. I always wanted to be better. One of the only ways I discovered I could do so was to study those who were considered the masters. I was always searching for more, wanting to learn more, discover more. My glimpses of valuable work is fleeting, and I don't have much access to the masterpieces themselves, but I try to take advantage when I have the opportunity."

"Well, now you do," Jonathan said. "You are welcome to visit this room anytime you'd like."

"Really?" she whirled around, her skirts flying about her so quickly that she nearly knocked over one of the marble pillars and she had to reach out to right it. "Are you sure? You don't have to. I—"

"Of course I don't have to," he said, straightening. "I can do as I please."

"Of course," she said, but she was so far across the room from him now that he wasn't sure whether she was mocking him or agreeing with him.

He began to cross the room toward her, indescribably drawn to her.

She was stopped in front of a Peter Paul Rubens.

"What do you think?" he asked, coming to stand next to her shoulder to shoulder as she stared at it.

"It's... thought-provoking," she said, her eyes glinting as she turned her head at an angle to better study it. Jonathan tried to see it through her eyes, but he was having a difficult time looking away from her. She was a picture of beauty in and of herself. So vibrant, so stunning, so full of life.

She wore her every thought on her face, and he wished he could find such an open honesty in himself.

"In what way?" he asked.

"You can tell the love depicted between the pair of them," she said, tilting her head, becoming lost in the painting. "There is honeysuckle — meaning love and lightness."

He swallowed, thinking of her own scent.

"He seems to be protecting her, guarding her, while the painting is so neat and orderly, as though their life is as well," she continued.

"It is a self-portrait, of the artist and his wife," Jonathan said softly. "You are a critic, Miss Donahue."

"Oh, I wouldn't say that," she shook her head as her cheeks turned pink. "I could never criticize someone so masterful."

"That's not what I meant," he said gently, not wanting to insult her. "I only meant that you see things others don't see, have a way of looking at the painting with an eye for detail, for emotion that most others would miss."

"Thank you." She dipped her head. "How do you come by all of these paintings?"

"Most of them through auction," he said as they continued on walking around the room, skirting the few chairs that dotted it. "Usually when some other bastard — excuse me — has lost his fortune and needs to sell them or when his estate has been forfeited to pay his debts."

"That's sad."

"It is," he agreed, "But it usually was due to a choice he made. To try to win his fortune at the gambling tables as opposed to hard work."

She turned to him, her eyes wide and serious. "Do you never gamble?"

"I do not."

She smiled then as she studied him. "No," she said, although she nodded as if in agreement. "You most certainly do not strike me as the gambling type."

"Meaning?"

"You see to be a man who enjoys certainty. Gambling is anything but."

"And you, Miss Donahue?"

"Oh, I don't have much opportunity to gamble. If I did... well, I suppose it would just be for a bit of fun."

"Fair enough," he said as they nearly completed their tour of the room.

"And just how did a man like you come to be so interested in art?" she asked, facing him with her head tilted to the side, a few thick black curls dangling from her temple. In most women, it would have been a deliberate style, but Jonathan had the feeling that for her, this was just how they fell, so naturally seductive, as was the rest of her.

"When I first became duke, I was a young man. Far too young. My father had not yet taught me all that I required. It was a heavy burden of responsibility." Jonathan stopped for a moment, having no idea why he was telling her all of this, but it seemed that once the words had started to flow, he couldn't hold them back. "I did my best, but I trusted the wrong people. There was a... family friend. I thought we had an understanding, in more ways than one." He wasn't quite ready to share that particular story. "Anyway, I was taken advantage of. From that day on, I vowed to make my own way in the world. The last thing I ever thought I would find some relief in was art, but I found myself visiting this room, filled with many of my grandmother's paintings. She also loved to paint herself. Being here brought me a strange sense of peace and joy I couldn't find anywhere else. So I kept collecting. Until we have this today."

Miss Donahue was staring at him as though he had grown a second head.

"What?" he asked gruffly, and she shook her head slightly in wonderment.

"I don't think I have ever heard you utter so many words at one point in time."

He laughed ruefully at that. "You are likely right."

"You should laugh more," she said, her eyes darkening as she smiled at him.

"Why?"

"Why not? Your entire face lights up," she said. "Do you not feel that same light in here when you do?"

She pointed to his chest, her finger nearly touching the front of his jacket.

"I suppose I feel something like that," he said slowly, not wanting to give her too much of himself.

She began to drop her finger, but before he could even think about what he was doing, he reached out and caught her gloveless hand in his.

She stilled, staring at their clasped hands in front of them.

"Miss Donahue," he said, his voice soft and low, but before he could continue, she reached up her other hand between them, holding it in the air to stop him.

"Calli."

"Pardon me?"

"Calli," she said, lifting her eyes to look up at him imploringly. "My name is Calli. You can use it... if you'd like."

"Calli," he repeated her, enjoying the roll of her name on his lips.

"Short for Calliope," she said, her eyes still on the wall of his chest in front of her.

"It suits you."

"Better than Miss Donahue?" she asked, a sad, rueful smile on her lips that he didn't quite understand.

"In moments like this, when it is just the two of us... it feels much more appropriate."

He bent his head closer to her, naturally inhaling the scent of honeysuckle that radiated from her. She was flowers and spring, light and love, everything that was missing in his life, everything that he didn't need — nor want.

Yet here she was.

"Your Grace..."

"Jonathan. If I am to call you Calli, I suppose you may call me by my given name as well. When the children are not about."

"Jonathan," she said, looking up at him with warm eyes,

and Jonathan had to admit that he had never heard his name upon lips so sweet before. "It is a lovely name."

This dance had been going on long enough. Before he could think any further on what he was doing or whether or not it was a good idea by any means, he leaned in and took those lips that were just begging for his kiss.

Calli stiffened for a moment in his embrace, as though she was in shock, but after a moment she relaxed into him, her lips moving under his, answering his every inquiry with a reply that told him she was equally as curious yet also as hesitant as he was.

But to hell with those questions, Jonathan thought before he let all thoughts flee, continuing his exploration.

She unclasped her hand from his, only to twine it with her own around the back of his neck, pulling him down closer, answering him with all of the enthusiasm he knew she would possess deep within her. He hesitantly reached out, clasping his hands around her waist. He was most certainly not a timid man, especially with women, but there was still that question as to whether or not he should be doing this with the woman he had hired as his governess.

But it seemed it was too late to back down now.

His fingers wandered of their own accord to wrap around her voluptuous hips, the ones he had been watching every time she walked out of a room. He deepened the kiss, slanting his mouth over hers until she opened to him, allowing his tongue inside to meet hers.

As much as she appeared the sultry vixen, it seemed that her sexiness was innate rather than practiced, for he could sense her innocence, which only fueled his desire for her. She was not, however, a woman who would ever back down, as evidenced by the way she met his strokes and tangled her tongue with his in a manner he would very much like to continue beyond the meeting of their mouths.

The thought was nearly enough to pull him from her embrace, until she pushed her ample breasts against him, and he was nearly a man lost. He broke from her, nipping her earlobe, kissing her neck, finding the pulse in her throat. How much he longed to continue the exploration, to push down the bodice of her gown, to throw her back against one of the plush velvet chairs in the corner of the room, to see what she looked like without all of the layers of her cheap clothing between them.

But he didn't. He couldn't. As much as every part of him was aching to do so.

It took every ounce of control he had worked on through his life — and he had built up quite a storage — to slowly pull himself back, away from the siren who seemed to break through his every defense and try to engrain herself deep within him. He placed one final kiss on the top of her head as though she were a child before he stepped back, turning around away from her, so that he didn't have to see her rosy cheeks nor her mussed hair nor her swollen lips — from *his* kisses.

"Jonathan?" she said softly from behind him as he ran a hand through his hair. "Are you all right?"

He barked out a laugh. He had never been better — had never felt more alive nor emboldened.

And yet he had also never been so completely out of control. This was madness.

"I apologize, Miss Donahue," he said, hearing the formality in his words, knowing how harsh and cruel they must sound to her. "I shouldn't have done that."

He heard her approach before he felt her hand tentatively touch his shoulder and he had to work not to flinch.

"Please, call me Calli," she said. "And never apologize for something like that. It was glorious."

She stepped around him, her feet hardly making a sound as she padded toward the door.

She turned and fixed her wide, direct gaze upon him.

"Thank you, Jonathan. For everything."

And at that, she was gone, slipping out into the corridor and leaving him in utter chaos.

CHAPTER 12

As soon as she was out of view from the door, Calli broke into a run, her hand against her lips, where she could still feel and taste Jonathan upon them.

Oh, God.

He had tasted wealthy. Like brandy and coffee and wonderfully like the duke he was.

Whereas she... she was stealing from him. He had literally found her breaking into his room of treasures, which he had then gone on to share with her.

She didn't deserve his trust, nor his kiss, nor his affection, nor his employ.

Arriving at her room, she threw herself on the bed, her head in her hands as she lay there, contemplating this mess she had found herself in.

When she had agreed to this, her role was supposed to have been to take a quick sketch of a painting. She was then to return home, where she would finish it and then allow Arie and Xander to do the rest.

Instead, here she was, wrapped up in this duke, in this family, unable to see her way out.

Knowing that there was little chance she would find sleep anytime soon, she locked the door before unrolling the canvas, which just fit across the expanse of floor that was not covered by any other furniture.

Calli arranged the paints in front of her before mixing them the color of the ocean that swept across the original canvas. It was so layered, the water moving in such great swirls of waves, that she knew it would be a challenge, but one she was up for. Her only concern now was how observant Jonathan would be over the painting. He seemed to have more knowledge on the subject than she had originally presumed. He was not a man who collected paintings for their value nor their prestige.

He didn't even showcase his most amazing pieces, but instead kept them hidden away from the world in a place for himself. It was a shame, and yet Calli could understand it.

She could only pray that the painting he housed in his study was one that he had become so used to seeing that he didn't even look at it anymore.

And when she left? Well, she would be nothing more than a memory for him. Hopefully a memory he looked back on with some fondness, if she did her job well and he never discovered her true intentions.

For if he ever did?

Well, she didn't even want to fathom it.

* * *

"Do you think she's dead?" Matthew's voice drifted into Calli's dreams.

Poke.

"I don't think so. Maybe she knocked her head." Mary. They were both here.

"On what?"

"How would I know?"

"If that was true, how did she get into her bed?" Matthew sounded indignant.

"Maybe she crawled."

"But wouldn't the light have woken her up?"

"I suppose…" Mary's confidence was waning.

"That's why I think she's dead."

Calli cracked her eyes open to see two matching, curious faces peering down at her.

"Oh, look, she's alive." Calli nearly laughed at how disappointed Matthew sounded.

"Thank goodness. I don't want Uncle to have to find a new governess." At least Mary was relieved.

"What time is it?" Calli groaned as she sat up straight in the bed, even as she brought a hand to her eyes to block the annoyingly bright sun that radiated through her south-facing window.

"I'm not sure, but we've already had breakfast."

"You have? How?"

"The maid left a tray."

"Why didn't she wake me?"

The children looked at one another and shrugged.

Calli sighed as she swung her legs over the side of the bed, hitting one of the containers of paint as she did. She had mixed them at home, knowing what colors she might need, and had then asked Xander to bring additional hues. She reminded herself to ask Xander to mix the final thin glazes for her when she returned to London. She tried to nudge the container under her bed with her toe, hoping the children wouldn't notice.

"What's that?" Mary asked, crouching, and Calli stood quickly, trying to distract her.

"What's what?"

"Whatever you just pushed under the bed."

"Nothing. Just a snack from last night."

"What were you eating?"

"I can't remember."

Why were children so relentlessly inquisitive? She couldn't understand how they didn't get through to their uncle. Their questions should be enough to wear anyone down.

Mary was faster than she, quickly reaching down and pulling the paint out from under her bed.

"Is this paint?"

"Ah… yes."

"Why do you have paint?"

"I enjoy painting," Calli said, deciding on the truth.

"Can we paint with you?"

Calli inhaled slowly, considering how much supply she had with her and how much the children might use. But one look at Mary's hopeful face told her she didn't have much choice.

"Of course. After I have my tea?"

They nodded and agreed to give her a few minutes to get dressed and prepare herself before joining them. After painting long into the night, Calli had only slept for a couple of hours. She couldn't keep this up or she was going to lose more than sleep — perhaps her sanity.

Tonight she would forgo painting for rest, she promised herself. But, until then, she had a long day to get through.

* * *

JONATHAN PULLED on his gloves as he began crossing the green to the stables, where he would find General and then go explore the lands he had been told about.

He didn't realize he was going to be waylaid.

"Uncle! Where are you going?"

He turned to find Mary and Matthew running up toward him.

"Children," he said stiffly with a nod. "Where is Miss Donahue?"

"She's sleeping," Mary said.

"Again," Matthew added.

"What do you mean, she's sleeping? It's noon." He looked around for the woman.

"She was reading to us under the big oak tree and then she fell asleep. We had to wake her up this morning, too."

Jonathan placed one hand on a hip as he rubbed the other hand over his forehead. Calli had been awake with him quite late last night, but she still should have found time for sleep.

"Show me where she is," he said with a resigned sigh.

"Why don't we come with you, instead?"

He gave them a look that told them he was not prepared for an argument.

"Fine," Mary said, kicking the toe of her boot into the ground before leading him across the grassy field toward the trees in the distance.

His smile began to form when he first spotted her, and only served to grow the closer they came.

For there, sprawled on a blanket under the large oak tree as comfortably as could be, was Calli. Fast asleep.

The three of them crouched down next to her, Matthew poking her in the side.

"She was like this when we woke her up this morning," he said, his words just above a whisper. "Barely moving. We thought she was dead."

She did look quite peaceful in her repose. She always carried an air of joy about her, but in sleep her tranquility was almost envious. Jonathan had the feeling that he never slept that soundly, instead always tossing and turning as he thought of all that was required of him the coming day.

"Should we let her sleep?" Mary asked, turning her head to look up at him, and Jonathan noted how much the girl looked like his sister. It was nearly disconcerting.

"I cannot leave you alone."

"We could come with you."

"I have to ride a fair distance."

"We know how to ride," Matthew said, pulling himself up to his full height, which was not actually that tall.

"Yes, but can you ride as fast as General?" Jonathan asked, lifting a brow, to which Matthew hung his head.

"No," he said ruefully. "No one can ride as fast as General, and I'm afraid I'm not tall enough to fit upon him." He looked up at Jonathan, hope in his eyes. "I could ride with you."

"And what of Mary?"

"I could take her."

They all jumped at Calli's voice, looking down to see that her eyes were now open and she was leaning up on her elbows.

"You're awake."

"Of course I'm awake," she said, her nostrils flaring indignantly, to which Jonathan couldn't help but laugh, and Calli and the children all looked at him wide-eyed with astonishment.

"Is something wrong?" he asked, looking between them all.

"You laughed," Mary said, her mouth slightly open, showing the gap between her teeth.

"Yes?" he said, not understanding.

"You never laugh," Matthew said, his little fists on his hips.

"Yes, I do."

"No, you don't."

"Sure, I do," he insisted, then hedged, "sometimes."

Calli took pity on him and began to push herself to her

feet. Jonathan held out a hand to help her, her fingers closing over his, causing a flood of memories from the night before to wash through him.

"You say you can ride, Miss Donahue?"

"Yes," she said, although her confirmation was far from sure.

"Did you ride much, growing up in London?"

"Now and then."

"Hmm," he said, looking at her and the firm tilt of her chin. "Very well. But you will ride Buttercup."

"Buttercup?"

"Yes, Buttercup. Come, then. Let's go before I change my mind."

* * *

CALLI WAS MORE than relieved to find that Buttercup was a rather old, sturdy, docile mare. Calli hadn't lied when she said she *could* ride, but she wasn't exactly skilled. She remembered riding a pony as a child, and when Arie's fortunes had grown enough to buy himself a horse, he had taught them each to at least lead the horse in a walk, should they ever find themselves in a situation that required it.

Well, here she was.

Mary settled in behind Calli, squeezing her little arms tightly around her, and Calli was suddenly gripped with how much responsibility she had taken on. The child's life was in her hands. Jonathan must have sensed her sudden unease, for as he handed Calli the reins, he placed his hands upon her clenched ones for a moment.

"Remember, the horse can sense your emotion. Be calm, and Buttercup will be calm as well."

She nodded, forcing herself to smile with a confidence she didn't quite feel.

Soon enough, however, they were walking slowly out of the stables, and Buttercup's steady rhythm provided Calli with assurance that even if she couldn't trust herself, she could, at least, trust the horse.

"That's it," she said, gently patting the horse on the neck as they followed Jonathan and Matthew upon General, a horse just as magnificent as his owner.

"How far are we going?" she called over to Jonathan as they caught up.

"To the next land over," he said. "We should only be gone for a couple of hours."

She nodded in response, although even a couple of hours atop a horse was a couple more hours than she had ever spent on one. She said nothing, however, but followed along behind, pleased, for the moment, to simply enjoy the beautiful day they had been gifted.

Now and again, she looked over at Jonathan, who seemed quite at home in the saddle. In fact, ever since they had arrived here at Wyndmere, he had slowly softened, losing some of the hard edge of his exterior that had surrounded him like a shell in London.

Perhaps it was the outdoors. Or maybe the fact that he was away from some of the responsibility that followed him around in the city.

Whatever it was, she enjoyed it. Perhaps too much.

For it was also far too easy for her to forget exactly why she was here in Jonathan's home. In London, her family made sure to constantly remind her, just in case she lost sight of what she was supposed to be doing.

Not so here in the country.

For goodness sake, she wasn't even thinking of him as the duke anymore, but as Jonathan. Which was incredibly dangerous. For the duke was an unattainable man, one who held far more wealth and prestige than was fair for any one man to have.

Jonathan was another entity altogether.

Especially a Jonathan who had agreed to take the children with him on an excursion. Matthew looked positively thrilled, his back straight and a wide smile on his face as he held onto his uncle. It was obvious how much he looked up to him, the man who was his family and the one person who had taken them in when they needed it the most.

"Miss Donahue?" Mary said from just behind her ear. "Can we go faster?"

Calli looked down warily at the reins she held ever-so-loosely in her hands.

"I'm not sure…"

"Please?"

Calli looked over at Jonathan, who must have heard, for he looked at her with brows raised and question in his blue eyes.

"We can go a little faster if you feel up to it."

She nodded determinately. "Of course."

She remembered Arie's teaching and nudged her heels softly into Buttercup's side.

It was obviously not nearly enough prodding, for Buttercup continued her slow, methodical pace.

"A little harder," Jonathan called, and Calli looked up to find a wide grin on his face. The man was laughing at her. She shot him a look of chagrin and nudged her heels in, much harder this time.

Buttercup obviously wasn't entirely pleased as she let out a slight whinny, but she listened this time, picking up her pace.

Jonathan urged General forward, and the two horses began an amiable trot together, nearly in unison.

Mary laughed in glee from behind Calli and Matthew

seemed similarly thrilled. Calli looked over at Jonathan, the two of them sharing a smile — one that they couldn't seem to break, nor could they look away from one another.

This feeling… the connection between them, the children, the horses, the sun upon their faces… it was better than anything Calli had ever known.

Which made the thought that it was fleeting only hurt that much more.

CHAPTER 13

*I*f only she wasn't so positively radiant. Then perhaps Jonathan would have been able to tear himself away from her.

But she practically drew him to her, as though there was some invisible rope around his waist that she kept tugging toward her, until he was caught with no wish to escape.

Jonathan had never thought that he would give any part of his heart away, nor hold affection for another. That didn't mean he wasn't going to marry. He was aware that he would be required to do so, for an heir if nothing else. He wished he could simply allow Matthew to inherit, but the laws of inheritance didn't work that way. If he didn't marry and have a son of his own, all of this — the land, the estate, the homes — that he had worked for would go to a cousin, one that by no means deserved it or would even know what to do with it.

At least Jonathan had amassed fortune enough from his investments in trade that he could one day leave a considerable amount to his niece and nephew. He would do right by them. He had promised his sister, yes, but it was as important to him as it would ever have been to her.

He had never considered, however, that he might allow himself to feel something for another woman. Especially not after Cecelia.

He rubbed a hand over his forehead. He had thought he had felt something for her, as well. Until he had realized that she was just using him.

In fact, he could hardly remember the last time he had dealings with anyone who wanted something from him besides what he could offer through his name and fortune.

But now there was Calli. A governess. A woman with no family name or connections. If he were to ever suggest something more serious to her than a bit of trifling in his gallery… what would that even look like? Oh, the scandal that would ensue. But did he even care?

"You look awfully solemn," Calli called over, jumping him out of his reverie. "Is everything all right?"

"Just fine," he said with a nod, although he kept his gaze ahead. They were arriving at the land he was considering, and he needed to be focused. He reined in General, and Buttercup was trained well enough to understand that she was to stop as well. They sat there at the edge of the land, overlooking the rest of it.

"Well?" he said, looking around at the rest of them. "What do you think?"

"It's very empty," Matthew said with a frown.

"That's a good thing," Jonathan said. "It can make for viable land. Miss Donahue, what do you think of it?"

Why her opinion mattered, he had no idea. But he couldn't stop himself from asking.

"I'm not sure what I'm supposed to think," she said, laughing uneasily. "I must be honest, Your Grace, I know nothing of land besides appreciation for the beauty of nature. As Matthew says, it is certainly wide open."

"Let's take a closer look," Jonathan said. "We'll see what it holds."

After a time, they dismounted and began walking the horses, as Jonathan inspected various areas to see what was currently growing, how damp the soil was and whether or not the land might be arable.

He could finally sense the children getting restless, and when they began to ask whether they had brought lunch, he somewhat regretted bringing them.

Until he remembered how pleased Calli seemed to be with the decision.

"We shall return to Wyndmere, and you can eat," he said, looking up at them. "I'm planning another trip here tomorrow and will speak more with the owner."

"Oh, good," Matthew said, and Jonathan couldn't help a small laugh at their obvious relief.

"Don't forget it was you who requested this journey."

"Yes, but I didn't realize how long it was going to be," Matthew grumbled a bit as Jonathan hoisted him back up on the horse after helping Calli and Mary.

"Patience, son," Jonathan said, and only when he had mounted himself did he sense the three of them staring at him once more.

"What's wrong?"

"Nothing," Calli said, shaking her head quickly, turning Buttercup around, but he didn't miss the smile that curled on her lips.

"You called me son," Matthew whispered, and Jonathan stilled. He hadn't even realized he had done so.

"I did," he said, unsure what to make of it himself.

"Thank you," Matthew said, laying his head against Jonathan's back. Jonathan's heart warmed, even as he had no idea just how to respond.

What in the devil was happening to him?

* * *

Calli hadn't forgotten her promise to allow the children to paint.

After returning to Wyndmere and ensuring they were well-fed, she led them up to the nursery, where she draped them in aprons that were far too large for them to ensure the paint didn't stain their clothing.

She unpacked her paint supplies and began to pour out a little bit for the children.

"A brush for each of you," she said, even as she bit her lip at the thought that if either of the brushes were damaged, she might have some difficulty completing her own painting.

But this was the decision she had made. The children deserved to have some fun with the pastime that brought her so much joy.

She pulled out her sketchbook, taking out a page for each of them to paint on.

"You can draw something first and then paint, or you can just paint," she said. "It is entirely up to you."

"What's the right way?" Mary asked, her paintbrush hesitating over the page.

"There is no right way," Calli said gently. "Art just is — let your heart paint for you."

"That makes no sense," Matthew said, looking at her somewhat critically, and Calli laughed.

"I know. But try anyway and perhaps one day you will understand."

"Will you paint too?" Mary asked, and Calli realized that they still weren't entirely sure what to do, that perhaps if she participated, they might be more at ease.

"Of course," she said, finding another brush and opening up her sketchpad to a blank page.

Inspired by their ride that morning, she dipped her paint

in the green and began to paint a landscape. She sensed the children following suit, and soon enough she was as lost in her work as she always was.

So much so that she didn't realize there was another presence in the room until Mary spoke out.

"Uncle! What are you doing here?"

Calli's head shot up, and she gasped in surprise when she found Jonathan standing in the doorway, arms crossed over his chest.

"I was walking by and heard you in here. Thought I would see what you were doing."

Calli narrowed her eyes. No other room in the house was near the nursery. But then she slowly widened them once more. He wanted to spend time with them — he just had no idea how to actually put that into words, and so he had made up his own excuse instead. It was actually somewhat endearing.

"Would you like to join us?" she asked, but he was already shaking his head.

"No, no."

He did, however, take a couple of hesitant steps into the room, coming to stand behind them, and Calli paused for a moment, unsure how to proceed with his close scrutiny.

Fortunately, he took a step away from her to see what the children were painting, and she followed his gaze with curiosity.

"Impressive," he said, and both children beamed at his compliment.

"It's the sun," Matthew explained, while Mary had a large heart in the center of hers.

"You are both fine artists," he said, before coming to stand behind Calli. "I can see why. For your teacher is most impressive."

She stilled, feeling the breath of his words on her neck, the warmth of his praise reverberating around her.

"It's just a landscape," she said with a shrug, but he touched her — just for a moment — on the shoulder.

"I have seen many paintings by masters, Miss Donahue, and this one has the makings to be as good as any of them."

Her cheeks warmed, even as she knew he couldn't possibly mean what he said.

He held out a hand to her. "May I see your other sketches?"

Her mind flew over what was contained within, and whether there was anything in the book that might tell him something about her that she didn't want him to know. She hesitated slightly, but seemed to remember removing everything she needed to and placing under her bed.

She tore out the freshly painted sheet and passed it over to him silently.

He didn't say anything, and all Calli could hear was the slip of one page to the next as he passed through her work. She felt open, exposed, as though he was looking within to see all that was inside of her.

Which was partially true. She poured her soul out into her sketches, into her painting. It wasn't often that she allowed another to see in.

"Thank you," he said softly when he handed it back to her after what felt like an indeterminable number of minutes. He must have understood her vulnerability at this scrutiny. "You are extraordinary."

Calli dipped her head, his words meaning more than he could ever imagine, even as Mary and Matthew giggled.

She cleared her throat, returning her attention to them. "And how are your paintings coming along?" she asked, which was enough to distract them as they proceeded to explain all of the thought they had put into them.

Jonathan walked to the door, pausing within the frame as he looked back, his expression too difficult to read as he looked at the children and then caught Calli's gaze. They stared at one another for a moment, caught, trapped, until he slid his hand back down and walked away, leaving Calli shaken — and longing to see him again.

* * *

Jonathan spent the night tossing in his bed, considering Miss Donahue — Calli. The woman he had kissed, the woman who was his governess, who worked for him, who he should be keeping as far away from as possible.

But what was he supposed to do when she refused to leave his thoughts? Stubborn woman.

Finally, he pushed aside the covers, rose from his bed, and went to the one place that always brought him solace — his gallery.

He stood in the entryway, looking around at the masterful works in front of him. He couldn't properly say just why he had begun such a collection. He had just realized that he enjoyed seeing the paintings, had appreciated the peace they brought him... and continued to collect.

The practical side of him knew that the money would be much better spent elsewhere, but fortunately he had amassed enough that he wouldn't particularly miss most of it.

And the paintings were investments in themselves.

"I thought I heard you."

He whirled around to find Calli standing in the doorway, a threadbare wrapper pulled tightly around her, bare toes poking out beneath. Her hair descended in waves as he always thought it might, and she looked like a Greek goddess — albeit a rather impoverished one.

Jonathan did all he could to keep his gaze on her eyes,

instead of dipping to the enticing beauty mark he longed to kiss, the plush lips that he yearned to taste again, and the flesh of her cleavage poking out just above the V of her nightgown.

"You heard me?"

"The corridor to the stairs runs alongside my bedroom," she explained simply.

"You couldn't sleep?"

"No," she shook her head, taking another step into the room. "I couldn't. As tired as I was."

He sighed, trying to think of every possible reason that might be cause for him to want to turn himself off, away from her, and back to the orderly life where he normally found himself.

There were many. But instead, he crossed the room, wrapped his hands around her hips, and pulled her toward him, hearing only her short gasp of surprise as he buried one hand in her hair, holding her against him with the other, and plundered her mouth with his.

CHAPTER 14

Was it possible for one's mind to completely stop functioning?

For Calli was sure that was what happened when Jonathan kissed her. All of her thoughts practicality fled, to be replaced only with emotion and a great need within her that longed to be answered.

She had stopped breathing when she saw the predatory look in his eyes as he strode across the room toward her, had no time to defend herself or draw back away from him.

Not that she wanted to.

She knew she should — she was stealing from the man, for goodness sake.

But everything within her told her that this — *he* — was right, and she had no choice but to surrender.

For it seemed that even if she had the capability to ration through this, her body had other ideas.

This time there had been no slow, careful exploration. Instead, it seemed as though he had been waiting for this — for *her* — and all of the pent-up passion inside of him came pouring out into her.

Calli found herself unabashedly responding.

She was not a complete innocent. Many men had wanted her, many men had tried. But none had stirred her enough for her to follow through. Any kisses she had accepted were sloppy, with boys who knew nothing of what they were doing.

Not like this man, who was as determined and as purposeful as he was with everything else he did.

Like she, he wore but a wrapper, and Calli slipped her hand underneath the fold of the robe to lay her fingers upon the hard planes of his chest. His warm skin was bristled with small hairs that only served to further arouse her every desire for him.

When his hand on her hip pulled her closer, Calli could feel the evidence of all that he wanted, and she wantonly ground herself against him, causing him to groan.

"Calli," he moaned as he lifted his lips slightly from hers, only to transfer his affections to her neck, and Calli stretched her head out to the side to allow him better access. He lifted her in his arms as though she weighed nothing, spinning her around before allowing her feet to settle down against the cold marble before he pushed her back against the wall.

He stretched an arm over her head, holding her there possessively, and when he bent her knee around his hip, she welcomed the pressure of him against her, wanting more of him, of this, even as she had no idea just what exactly that would mean.

Why had she even come here? The hazy thought formed in the back of her mind. Oh yes, because she was drawn to the sound of his footsteps, pulled like she had no other choice.

The thought mattered no longer, however, as Jonathan trailed kisses down her shoulder, over her collarbone as Calli remembered him doing before, but this time she was not wearing a dress that offered no flexibility.

Her nightgown was high but thin, and when he pushed the wrapper out of the way, she knew her breasts would be on full display for him through the thin white material of her nightgown.

His swift intake of breath, however, seemed to communicate that he had no cause for complaint, and as her wrapper fell completely open, he lifted one breast and then the other in his hands, before he bent his head and suckled one nipple through the fabric of her nightgown as he tweaked the other with his fingers. Calli moaned, her head falling backward, her shoulders pushing her breasts closer toward him, offering them to him, practically begging for more.

She didn't know what exactly she was asking for, but Jonathan seemed to be well aware.

With her knee around his hip, her nightgown was already spread open for him, and his fingers wrapped around her ankle in a vise. He trailed them up her calf, sparking sensations through nerves that she didn't even know were possible to cause such tremors.

His fingers continued to wander as his ministrations were relentless, and Calli felt like an instrument at the mercy of a powerful musician.

He finished the journey up her thigh quickly, his fingers finding her, stroking her, causing her to cry out and jerk upward away from him — only for her to settle back down, welcoming him once more.

"Is this all right?" he asked, looking up at her with eyes glazed over in desire, and she returned his stare, unsure if she would be able to properly form words.

"Y-yes," she managed. "Of course."

He stroked her again and again, refusing to abandon her breasts at the same time, and before Calli knew what was happening, the heady sensation of her release began to build, until it rocketed through her with a force she never could have expected.

She was sure her cry could be heard through the entire house, until Jonathan silenced it by placing his mouth back upon hers, kissing her until the waves became small ebbs.

Calli shuddered as she collapsed in his arms, shaken — by the experience, by the intensity… by Jonathan.

"Are you all right?" he murmured, holding her close against him.

"Better than all right," she said hoarsely. "That was… that was…"

"I know," he said, and Calli could have sworn he was laughing slightly. The man who never laughed would laugh now after *that*?

She leaned back, looking up into his face as he stared back at her with a warmth that rather unsettled her.

"Time for sleep," he said, leaning down and kissing her briefly, chastely, on the lips.

As though she could sleep after that.

"But—" she began, reaching for him, knowing he must be aching, but he stepped away from her.

"Another time," he said softly. "You need to sleep. Can't have the governess napping away the day under a tree again."

Calli flushed, although whether her cheeks could turn any redder than they likely already were, she had no idea.

"I am so sorry," she said, her words just above a whisper. "I never meant—"

He placed his index finger against her lips.

"I know. I wasn't criticizing."

Calli swallowed hard, nodding, wanting to stay here, with him, yet unsure what she was supposed to say or do — which wasn't at all like her. Usually, she knew exactly how to respond in nearly every situation.

"Jonathan, I—I'm not sure what this is, but—"

"Calli," he murmured, "I don't know either, but I don't think we need to put words to it right now. We enjoy being together. I feel a passion for you I don't think I ever have for another. But I don't want to take advantage of you."

Calli dipped her head. "It is not taking advantage when both people welcome it."

He laced his fingers through her hair, tilting her head back up toward him.

"That is a welcome sentiment, for certain," he said. "But even still. You are the governess and it wouldn't be right for me to take liberties. Beyond what I already have."

She was the governess. Right. He wouldn't ruin her, but nor would he ever take a step forward with her.

And she shouldn't want to! She was forgetting why she was even here, what she was doing to him. Somehow this identity she had assumed was becoming far too real. She had to remember who she was, where she came from, and what her family expected of her. To do anything else would only be setting them all up for disaster.

"Right," was all she murmured, as she stepped back away from him, trying to ignore the warmth that spread through her as he pulled together the front of her wrapper before tying the belt around her waist. "Good night then."

"Good night, Calli," he said so softly, so gently, and before Calli could talk herself out of it, she turned around and fled the room.

* * *

JONATHAN WASN'T surprised when he walked out to the stables the next day only to find two shadows beginning to trail behind him.

He didn't turn around as he asked, "yes?"

"Where are you going?" Matthew asked, and Jonathan had to bite the inside of his cheek to hold in his chuckle.

"Business," he responded. "Where is your governess?"

"She's coming," Mary said. "She wasn't fast enough."

Sure enough, there was Calli, running across the expanse of green after them, her skirts in one hand, her other arm swinging back and forth beside her. She wore a soft green today that was lovely on her, causing her hair to shine and her eyes to gleam as she approached.

"Children," she said between heavy breaths, "please don't leave me like that."

Matthew and Mary giggled behind raised hands as they looked at one another before sneaking a glance at Jonathan as though determining the severity of his ire.

"She's slow," Mary observed.

They laughed as Calli rolled her eyes.

"We were picking apples," she explained. "I turned around and they were gone."

"Uncle Jonathan is leaving on business," Matthew said.

"We want to come," Mary added.

"You can't come," Jonathan cut in, finishing their protestations.

"Why not?" they asked together.

"Because it is business." He sighed, unable to keep the impatience from his tone. "I can't show up inquiring about a man's land with my niece and nephew and governess in tow."

Although even as he said it, he couldn't properly look at Calli, remembering all that had transpired between him and this governess just last night.

All that should never have happened and yet it had felt more right than anything he had ever experienced before. What was it about this woman that caused him to forget everything he always held so important?

"Please, Uncle?" Mary said, cutting through his musings. "We will be very quiet and stay outside if you wish."

"Yes, we are bored," Matthew, said, dragging out the last word, even through Calli's snort of indignation.

"Is Miss Donahue not keeping you entertained?" he asked, lifting a brow as he attempted to keep his smile subdued.

"Well, yes, but Matthew just means we are bored not going anywhere else, seeing the same walls again and again," Mary said, and Jonathan laughed when Calli rolled her eyes behind the children.

"Heaven forbid you are relegated to an estate such as this one with nowhere else to go," Jonathan said, then looked between the two of them and their earnest expressions.

"Fine," he said, to which they cheered in excited and shocked surprise. "But you must listen to me and to Cal—Miss Donahue, and if there is any hint of misbehaviour, this shall be the last time I ever allow such a thing, do you understand?"

"We understand!" they shouted as they ran to prepare themselves for the quick trip.

Calli studied him for a moment with a raised brow before she turned and followed her charges.

Jonathan prepared himself for a long ride.

CHAPTER 15

Jonathan had decided that today they would stay to the roads, so while Calli was a bit disappointed not to see the open land she had enjoyed on their last ride, at least the terrain was slightly easier to navigate, particularly with Mary holding on behind her.

They hadn't gone far, however, when the children spied buildings in the distance.

"Uncle!" Mary called, causing Calli to wince when the girl screamed in her ear. "What is that?"

"Over there?" Jonathan responded, lifting a hand to shade his eyes. "The village."

"I've never been to the village before," Mary said, this time not quite as loudly but still with a great deal of interest. Calli herself was somewhat intrigued. She had spent her life in London, but not much time anywhere smaller. What would such a place be like?

"We don't have time," Jonathan said, already anticipating the children's question.

"Please?" Matthew said. "Just for a few minutes, can we see what's there?"

Calli was sure Jonathan was going to say no, which is why she raised her brows at his assent, as begrudging as it was.

The four of them on horseback were certainly quite the draw for onlookers as they began to plod through the small town, that was as sleepy as Calli might have imagined it to be. People stepped out of doorways to watch them go by, most of them with a smile and a friendly wave that Calli and the children returned. They had only been riding a few minutes when they approached what seemed to be the village's largest buildings.

"What are those, Uncle?" Matthew asked.

"There is a small inn with the general store beside it," Jonathan explained, his voice as unattached as he was to most things.

"Can we go into the store?" Mary asked eagerly, likely already anticipating sweets.

"For just a moment," Jonathan said, apparently realizing that he had lost the battle before it began and therefore chose not to fight. Calli turned her head to hide her smile.

Jonathan pulled open the obvious heavy wooden door, allowing them through. The light was dim inside the store, small windows allowing a bit of sunlight to filter through, shining on the dust motes in the air as well as the food stores on the shelves.

Mary immediately found the sweets, of course — she seemed to have a nose for sniffing out sugar — and Jonathan pulled out coin for them as Calli watched with her arms crossed and a smile on her face.

She was so enamored with the scene in front of her that she was completely taken off guard when a hand grabbed her arm and pulled her behind a shelf.

"Xander!" she hissed when his familiar face came into focus. "What are you doing?"

"What am I doing?" he whispered with raised brows. "What are you doing? Playing house with the duke?"

"Yes, that is exactly what I'm doing," she said, crossing her arms over her chest. "Playing governess, anyway. Now, why are you here in Kent?"

"Arie sent me to look after you," he said, his voice low, his eyes flicking up to look behind her now and again. "He was worried when you left London."

"I can take care of myself," she said indignantly. If it had been Xander who had left on an assignation, no one would have pursued him to watch over him.

"I know you can, but you… well, Calli, you have a heart like none of the rest of us do, so you can understand why Arie might be worried."

Calli tried to push away thoughts of herself in Jonathan's arms, worried that Xander would be able to read the guilt on her face if she let them invade.

"I am keeping to the job," she promised with what she hoped was a convincing nod.

"Good," he said. "Well, I'll try to come by the estate and check in on you. I could hardly believe when I looked out the window of my bedroom and saw you riding through town, sitting high on your horse like a princess herself."

Calli laughed a bit too loudly at that as Xander looked around her.

"Hardly," she said, tempering herself, "although I am glad now that Arie insisted on the riding lessons."

"You best go," Xander said, nodding beyond her. "But be careful, Calli. Look after yourself. Where are you going?"

"To a neighbouring estate. A baron's, I believe."

"Ah," Xander's features lit up with interest. "I've heard of the man. He has quite the collection of Greek statues. Steal one for Arie. He would be most appreciative."

"But—"

"Miss Donahue?"

Calli whirled around to find Jonathan looking at her with some concern.

"Were you speaking to someone?"

"I—"

Calli turned back around, but found that Xander had disappeared.

"Just talking to myself," she said, forcing a smile.

"We bought you a sweet!" Mary said, skipping over toward her and holding out a red candy.

"Thank you," Calli said to Mary, unable to look up at Jonathan, once again wishing that her emotions were not so easily read. But Jonathan didn't seem to notice as he turned and beckoned them forward. Calli took one more look behind her, seeing only the back of a familiar head of black hair browsing the shelves. She swallowed and then followed Jonathan and the children out the door.

* * *

"Do you promise that you will all stay outdoors in the yard?" Jonathan asked, looking at the three of them with question as he dismounted his horse.

"Of course," Calli said with a quick nod, her expression making it clear that she did not entirely appreciate being spoken to as though she was one of the children. "I will keep a good eye on them."

"I know you will."

A groom approached and took the horses as Jonathan walked to the front door, looking back to see the children already racing across the grass, Calli in their wake. Ah, but to have such energy.

"Your Grace?"

When he turned the butler was waiting for him, and he

walked through the door to find the baron already sitting in the front parlor.

"Your Grace, welcome. I couldn't help but notice through the window of my study that you are not alone today. Perhaps you would like your wife and children to come inside as well? My grandchildren are in residence, and they might enjoy some company."

"My—oh. My niece and nephew. And that is not my wife. The governess," Jonathan said, even as heat began to rise from his stomach, up through his chest and into his face at the very thought of Calli being so attached to him.

"My apologies, Your Grace. She is such a beautiful woman, I could only assume. Still, they are of course invited in."

"Ah, yes, thank you," Jonathan said, slightly thrown still by the idea the baron had put forth.

"Very good. I shall have my butler approach them. Come with me to my study."

He held his arm out, and Jonathan followed him toward the door he pointed to. "I trust you have had the opportunity to see the lands that I would like to sell?"

"I have," Jonathan said with a nod. "May I ask why you would like to be rid of them?"

The elderly Baron Chilton sighed as he settled his considerable frame into the chair behind the desk.

"My son… he is a good boy, but not entirely responsible. He likes the gaming tables."

The baron looked down morosely for a moment, not needing to say anymore. "I suppose I need some of the funds to pay off his debts. It is not ideal, but—?" He raised his hands in the air.

Jonathan looked past him to the walls of the office and the statues that lined the shelves.

"You have a fair bit of artwork that could be sold off, do you not?"

The baron steepled his fingers together in front of him.

"I do," he said with a nod. "You have a good eye. But the truth is, Your Grace, I am not getting any younger, and my son, well, I'm not sure how the lands will fare under his leadership. I am concerned for the wellbeing of the people, the animals, the land itself... It might be best under the hand of someone who knows what he is doing. My son has never cared enough to pay any attention."

"Fair point," Jonathan said, respecting the man's honesty as well as his dedication to his tenants and the people who worked for him. It was not often one saw such commitment that he was willing to give up part of his own property to ensure the welfare of others.

Footsteps suddenly pounded overhead, interrupting them, and the man's worried face eased into a smile. "My grandchildren," he said. "It seems they have found your niece and nephew. Good of you to bring them."

Jonathan thought of their pleading for him to do so, and managed a nod. "Of course."

"Your man of business likely provided you with my thoughts on what I'd like for the land," the baron said. "Now the question is, what do you think it's worth?"

The two of them began negotiations, and before long, they were standing, shaking hands after coming to an agreement that they both seemed to be pleased with.

"Would you like to see my gallery?" the baron asked, light entering his eyes, and Jonathan nodded.

"Very much so."

The baron's "gallery" was not so much a shrine to the art such as Jonathan's own room, but was more so a parlor or sitting room that had been redesigned to accommodate his many statues, all of which appeared to be Greek in origin.

"Fascinating," Jonathan said as he wandered the room, reminding himself of Calli when she had first entered his own gallery. "Where did you come by most of these sculptures?"

"Some were brought back to England by Elgin himself," the baron said, raising his bushy eyebrows.

"With the Elgin marbles?"

"The very ones," the baron said, his eyes gleaming, "although most of them ended up in the Museum. Others I have accumulated over the years, from other collectors, or from those who have gone on acquisition trips."

"I see," Jonathan said. "How have you organized them?"

"By date of origin, or at least, by date as well as we can determine," the baron said, placing his hands on his hips as he looked around him with a sigh. "Unfortunately, my collecting days may be at an end for now, but I will do what I can to look after what I have. And, in the meantime," he said as he turned to Jonathan with a twinkle still in his eye, "I have made sure that my *daughter* is the one who will look after them once I am gone."

Jonathan grinned at that, wishing for a moment that he could give away his own inheritance as he wished and not as how he was entitled to by law and tradition. Although he supposed he was no different than the baron — he could do as he wished with anything not entailed.

He was nearly finished his perusal of the room when he came to the final shelf, closest to the door.

"What used to be here?" he asked, pointing to a circle where it seemed a statue had used to stand. "Did you have to sell something off?"

"I've sold nothing off," the baron said before lumbering across the room. "Where?"

Jonathan showed him, and the baron's expression lost all

signs of a twinkle, his countenance growing rather irate as his face reddened.

"There should be a statue here of Perseus," he said, looking around as though Perseus was going to jump out from behind a pillar nearby. "Where is it?"

"I'm not sure," Jonathan said, uncertain of just whether or not he was supposed to answer that question. "Perhaps it was moved for cleaning?"

"No one touches my collection except for my butler," the baron said. "I trust no one but the man who has been with me the longest. One slight hit by an errant duster from a new maid, and thousands of pounds could be shattered to the floor in a moment."

Jonathan also thought that the pieces of history that would be scattered might also elicit a reason to be wary, but he didn't feel that it was his place nor the time to say anything.

"Perhaps the butler knows then," Jonathan said as the baron went out to the corridor, calling for the man.

The butler, however, seemed as bewildered as the two of them.

"Well," the baron said, raising his hands in the air, "I am sorry to end our visit on such a note. At least everything else went quite well and I thank you, Your Grace, for coming all this way."

As though on cue, the children appeared from upstairs, their faces red but their manners intact.

"We are ready to depart," Jonathan said to Mary, Matthew, and Calli, who all nodded, and Jonathan couldn't help but note the baron's appreciation for Calli as she walked by. Even though he was well aware that there was nothing to fear from the man, nor that Calli might potentially be interested in someone old enough to be, at the very least, her father, he still questioned just where this jealousy had come from and whether or not it was warranted. It was most certainly not welcomed.

"You shall hear from my man of business regarding the particulars," Jonathan said before leaving. "And best of luck in locating your statue."

The man nodded, and Jonathan greeted the fresh air with a smile.

It had been a good day, indeed.

CHAPTER 16

Calli couldn't seem to properly hold onto anything that night at dinner. Every utensil seemed to practically fall out of her fingers, she nearly dropped the gravy bowl, and then she succeeded in spilling drops of red wine on her dress, which was, thankfully, a dark navy tonight.

"Is there anything amiss, Miss Donahue?" Jonathan asked from the head of the table, looking at her inquisitively.

"No, nothing at all," she said with what she hoped was a breezy tone. "Just tired, I suppose, from the riding today."

"I wouldn't have taken you if I had realized how taxing it would be," Jonathan said, causing Calli to receive twin glares of ire from her charges.

"Nothing to worry about," she said, willing the conversation to move elsewhere.

She wasn't so lucky.

"You seem to need more sleep, Miss Donahue," Jonathan said. "Best be to bed early tonight."

"Of course, Your Grace," she said with a nod, as she stared at the plate in front of her, her only actions at the moment moving the food around her plate, hoping it would seem that she was eating.

But her entire appetite had fled. She was far too unsettled, far too unsure, far too caught between two worlds, neither of which seemed to completely embrace her.

She had made a decision in the space of a moment, and now she had no idea whether or not she had done the right thing.

Only she had the sense that, from the guilt that hung upon her like a cloak of doom, it had been very, very wrong.

Calli had only ever wanted to be accepted by her family, regarded to be as good as the rest of them, as willing and as capable. Yet she had always been relegated to the sidelines — the decoy, the lookout; that had been all she was good for. Until now.

Remembering Xander's visit, Arie's words, all of the expectations placed upon her and the fact that she had, so far, failed miserably, when she had seen the room of statues in the baron's estate, she had acted nearly without thought.

The weight of that little statue in her pocket had been dragging her around ever since.

She knew what Arie would say to her guilty thoughts — that the room of Greek treasures no more belonged to the baron than it did to any of them. That the relics of his homeland belonged back in Greece. Never mind that Arie would likely sell them to the highest Greek bidder without a shred of guilt in doing so as he pocketed the money, but only to a Greek bidder would they go.

No, her guilt didn't lie there. Her guilt lay in the fact that she had betrayed Jonathan's trust, had entered the baron's house as one of Jonathan's family — even if she was part of the family of staff — and had deceived him.

Even though, in the end, she was only here to betray him in a way far more personal and to a much greater extent.

"Miss Donahue?"

Calli blinked a few times, coming back to the present to see Jonathan and his niece and nephew all staring at her inquisitively.

"Yes?"

"We said your name about five times," Matthew complained, and Calli shook away her doubts.

"I'm so sorry. What was it you needed?"

"Uncle was telling us about his plans."

"Oh?" She looked up at Jonathan to find that he was gazing at her intently, as though he could unlock all of her secrets with that stare of his. If he ever did... Calli was finished.

"We will be returning to London," he said, keeping his eyes on her, as though determining what her reaction might be.

"We will?" Calli asked, trying to keep her expression neutral. She knew she should be celebrating the fact. It would mean that she could ensure the accuracy of her painting, that she could meet with her family if necessary, and that she was that much closer to finishing this entire charade and returning to her life.

And yet... she didn't want this to end. She was enjoying herself far too much, with Jonathan, and with the children. Children who had started this journey trying to trick her, and a man who she never thought she would ever see smile. Now, their joy and their smiles were all that she seemed to care for, while thoughts for her own family came secondary.

What was becoming of her?

"My business here is concluded," Jonathan said, taking a sip of his wine but not removing his eyes from her. "I must return to Parliament."

"Will we come back to Wyndmere, Uncle?" Matthew asked earnestly, and Calli could understand why the children so loved it here. The house was spacious, and the grounds provided ample space for the children to play and ride and climb trees. In addition to enjoying their time with the baron's grandchildren, Matthew and Mary had met the neighbor's children who were near to the same age, and Calli could see them spending much time together.

"Yes, after the Season, I think we should return for a time," he said, smiling at Calli. "What do you think Miss Donahue?"

Calli started, realizing he was almost... consulting with her. "I think that would be lovely," she said softly, even as she realized she would not be here with them. She would be gone by then. And they would hate her.

"Good," he said, his lips curling up into a rather seductive smile just for her, and at the flare of his nostrils and the gleam in his eyes, a shudder shook through Calli, knowing just what he was thinking of.

More time for the two of them. Alone.

Suddenly she desired it with every part of her being. If what Jonathan had done for her the other night was a taste of what would come if he was to ever fully make love to her... then she might not be able to handle it.

She swallowed hard, finally wrenching her eyes away from him, unable to meet his stare any longer. For what was she to do? Once he discovered who she truly was and what she was doing here with him, he would want nothing more to do with her.

But he didn't know. Not now. And if everything went according to Arie's plan, he never would.

Perhaps... she toyed with the stem of her wine glass. Perhaps she should allow to happen what they both so obviously wanted. Was that incredibly selfish? Would he hate her even more? Or would it be the one thing she could give him, when she would be taking everything else away?

She sighed. There was no right answer. There never was.

* * *

JONATHAN KNEW SOMETHING WAS WRONG. Calli was many things — exuberant, eager, easily pleased. But she was never this melancholy ghost of herself. He wouldn't normally care. It shouldn't be any of his concern. As long as his employees did the job they were hired to do, that was all that mattered to him.

Except for Calli. Calli had come to matter. She had found her way into a heart that he thought had long turned itself off to any potential affection for another.

He sighed as he paced in front of her bedchamber. He assumed the children were sleeping, and he remembered his own advice for her to retire early. But he needed to talk to her. Finally, he stepped up and knocked ever so lightly on the door.

It took her so long to answer that he wondered for a moment if she was even within. But then the door finally opened a crack, and she peeked her head out. All he could see was one sliver of her face, and an abundance of curl.

"Calli?" he whispered. "You weren't sleeping, were you?"

"No," came her response, before she pulled the door open just wide enough that she could step out into the hall. "Is there something amiss?"

"No. Yes. I—"

He was sounding like a youth in the first blush of love. He sighed. "It seemed there was something wrong at dinner. I wanted to make sure that you were well."

She seemed surprised as she nodded. "I am. My apologies. It's nothing to be concerned with."

"But there is something."

She looked down for a moment before staring back up at

him, and it took Jonathan another few seconds to realize the emotion that was swimming within her eyes.

Desire.

"I want you," she said, her voice hoarse at the words that she didn't seem to fully believe herself. "Desperately. And I don't know what to do about it."

Jonathan nearly fell backward at her revelation. He had felt it the other night, had known she would have been willing for more, but he had been sure that she would never act upon it. He had been equally sure that it would be the wrong thing to do, that he should be the responsible duke he was and not allow his own near-unbridled passions to sully another.

He closed his eyes, trying to summon all of the control that Calli was attempting to undo.

"Calli, I—"

Before he reopened his eyes, however, she had launched herself into his arms, nearly pushing him back against the wall behind him, and his arms instinctively wrapped around her, holding her close, as he attempted to both talk and kiss her back at the same time.

"I'm not sure this is a good—"

But she was kissing him again, and Jonathan sighed, giving into her lips, which seemed to have learned quite quickly just what they were supposed to be doing.

"Calli," he groaned into her mouth, before reason, if not enough to stop him entirely, spoke up loudly enough to remind him that they were in the middle of a corridor and that anyone — servant or child — could easily walk in and discover them.

"We can't do this here," he said, and she looked up at him, nodding. As he tried to back her up into her room, however, she shook her head.

"Not in there. It is far too close to the children," she said. "Your chamber?"

"I—" He would take her there, talk to her, and they would determine a way forward. Yes, that is what they would do. "Very well."

She took his offered hand, and he led her through the hall and then down the stairs, taking each turn surreptitiously to ensure that no one was about. Thankfully, most, if not all, of the sparse staff would have retired by now. He had sent his valet to bed ages ago.

Having no other adults in the house was a benefit for such times, as it would mean, at least, there were no other lady's maids or valets who might still be awake at such an hour.

Finally, he opened his chambers' door, allowing her in, and she quickly caught his attention with her gasp of surprise.

"Calli, what's wrong?" he asked, next to her in a moment.

"Nothing, it is just that painting... it is incredible."

"Ah, yes," he said, standing back and appreciating it, realizing that some of the paintings in his homes had been adorning the walls for so long that he often forgot to notice them any longer. A pity, for they did bring much beauty and joy into his world. "I have a similar one in my London study. He enjoyed painting people, but I wish he had done more landscapes. His painting of the sea is magnificent, and there will never be another like him."

"Right," Calli said, the word slightly strangled, and he turned to look at her, noticing for the first time that she still wore her gown, not yet changed into her nightclothes.

"Are you sure you are all right?"

"I am," she said, stepping toward him with a small smile, and he couldn't help himself from tucking a stray lock of hair behind her ear. "I just… I'm not sure how to reconcile these feelings I have for you… with my place in life."

"As a governess."

"Right. As a governess."

"It is difficult when you are the most beautiful governess I have ever seen."

She laughed at that, even as he stepped closer.

"Beautiful, and kind, compassionate, and so intelligent that you have even managed to outwit my most cunning niece and nephew."

"Oh, I wish you wouldn't say such things about me," she said, biting her lip, and he furrowed his brow.

"Why not? It's all true."

"It's not," she said, shaking her head, and he ran a hand down her face.

"If I say it is," he said with all of the determination running through him, "It is."

To prove his point, he kissed her then, hard and unrelenting.

Looking back, that was probably the moment he lost himself to her.

CHAPTER 17

With that kiss, Jonathan proved to Calli that he was the right man — for her first time, for her next time, for her last time. But since now was all that they would ever have, she would take it — without regrets.

She returned the passion of his kiss with wild abandon, deciding that she would let go of all her reservations and embrace all that Jonathan and this night had to offer.

He sank his hands into her hair, his fingers gripping her scalp as he held her head tilted up toward him while he feasted on her mouth. Their tongues tangled in mutual assault that was just as much a promise of what more there was to come. Calli welcomed the taste of brandy and chocolate on his tongue, and were this any other situation, she would have laughed to know that even His Grace indulged in a sweet now and again.

Although she supposed that was what he was doing right now.

He broke from her mouth as abruptly as he had claimed it, his breathing ragged as he continued to hold her head in his hands, while he now stared deeply into her eyes.

"Calli," he said, his voice husky with desire, "if we do this, I—I don't know what promises I can make, or what I can keep, and I never give my word unless I know with the utmost certainty I can uphold it."

Calli nodded. She knew all of this, and as much as she wished they lived in a different world, one in which she was a woman who would be worthy of him, for far more reasons than the difference in their stations, this was the way it had to be.

"I understand," she said softly.

"I don't want to ruin you," he said, uttering a curse, and Calli smiled sadly.

"You've already ruined me for every other," she said, "for there is no other man I shall ever want with as much desperation as I want you."

"So be it," he groaned before backing up toward the bed, taking her hand and pulling her along with him.

The room was grand, Calli dimly noted through the haze of her thoughts. One huge, beautiful painting of a sunset that looked as though it belonged just outside the window was the only adornment on the largest wall, while the fire from the ornate marble hearth on the opposite side of the room danced light upon the planes of Jonathan's chiseled face.

The bed itself was nearly as big as Calli's entire bedroom at home, thick green canopies cascading down from above them. Calli felt as though she was entering a forbidden inner sanctuary, the thought causing her pulse to race even faster than it already was.

Jonathan kept his eyes on her as he began to unbutton his jacket, throwing it to the side with a casualness most unlike him. Calli was suddenly quite grateful for Diana's forethought to pack dresses that she was able to fasten and unfasten herself, and she reached around her back for the overly large buttons.

"No," Jonathan said, shaking his head with command. "Let me."

He swiftly stepped around her, behind her, his fingers making deft work of the buttons, although he didn't push the dress down over her shoulders — not yet, apparently. His cravat and his waistcoat followed his jacket, and Calli couldn't imagine anything more seductive than the scene in front of her.

She stepped up, unable to keep herself from participating any longer, and began to slip the buttons out of the holes of his linen shirt.

He said nothing, though Calli could feel his gaze upon her. When she was finished, he pulled it up, over his head, and Calli took a moment to appreciate the sight in front of her. She had felt the skin of Jonathan's chest before, but she hadn't realized just what was awaiting her. He looked like the Greek statues she had admired in the baron's parlor — chiseled perfection, although much more alive, as his chest pumped up and down in time with his rather quick breaths, and Calli placed a hand over his heart to feel it beat against her palm.

"Wondering whether it works?" he asked, his voice gruff yet laced with a bit of laughter.

"I know it does," Calli said softly. "I just wanted to feel its strength."

He didn't respond, but kissed her again, his hands sweeping down her back as he now pushed the dress down over her shoulders, leaving her in her stays and her chemise.

His hands encircled her waist before he removed the stays with an ease that caused Calli to wonder how many times he had done so before, but soon she didn't care, for he had pulled her against him and she could feel the wondrous heat of his body along the entirety of her torso.

Jonathan scooped her up, turning around with her in his

arms until he deposited her on the bed, and in the moment between when he left her there and then returned to her, she missed his closeness with a ferocity that scared her.

But soon enough, he was back, his hands sweeping over her face as though she was one of his priceless treasures.

"You are the most beautiful thing I have ever seen," he whispered with awe, and Calli's eyes widened.

"I'm sure you've seen — been with — women far more beautiful."

"Never," he said, before dropping a kiss on her beauty mark, one that Diana told her was enticing but that Calli had always wanted to be rid of. He trailed kisses down her face, over her shoulder, pushing down the strap of her chemise, covering the now-bared skin with his kisses.

He repeated the gesture over and over, inching the chemise down one fingerbreadth at a time, following with his mouth.

Calli moaned and arched up into him when he reached her breasts, but after one quick kiss on each he continued downward. He completely ignored the very place she ached for him — deliberately, she was sure — and followed with kisses over her hipbones to her knees, where she never knew such sensitive places lurked, and down until he placed one last kiss on her ankle.

"You're a tease," she hissed, and when he reared up before her, his eyes were dark.

"Am I?"

"You are," she said. "Come here and kiss me properly."

He did just that, kissing Calli until she could barely think straight, until she hardly remembered who she was anymore.

Which was just fine with her.

His hands danced over her body as he played with her mouth, as she arched up toward him, needing more but unsure of just exactly what that more was.

He knew, though.

Finally, one of his hands found the very place she wanted him, his thumb coming to the bundle of nerves, rubbing, circling, teasing, as he slipped one finger into her, and then another. Calli knew from last time what magnificence he could evoke from his hand, but she wanted more, and she lifted her head away from him and told him so.

"Very well," he said. "Whatever you say."

Calli realized then that he was still wearing his breeches, and he sat up and away from her, undoing the fastenings before inching out of them.

She could only stare.

Yes, she had seen many statues and paintings and was no stranger to what the male form looked like.

But never had she seen it in... well, in such glory.

When she returned her gaze to Jonathan's, he was smirking as though he recognized her appreciation, although she also held a fair bit of concern.

"So, ah, what is the plan?" she asked, uncertainty and longing at war.

"For once, Calli," he said, dropping down next to her so she could no longer see him, his breath hot against her ear, causing her to shiver, "there is no plan. We just do what feels right."

"Very well," she said, the words so quiet she almost didn't hear them herself.

"And if something doesn't feel right," he continued, "then we stop."

She could only nod.

He kissed her as he settled between her thighs, her legs parting for him as though they already knew what to do. Her hips arched up to him, and he eased himself forward until she could feel him at her entrance. Then he slowly, gently, pushed into her, and Calli froze for a moment at the intrusion.

Jonathan seemed to understand as he didn't rush things, pausing and then resuming, until he was fully seated within her.

And then Calli didn't feel so frozen anymore.

"All right?" he asked, his words guttural as a bead of sweat broke out on his brow, and Calli nodded, clutching his shoulders so hard she wondered whether she would leave indents in his skin.

He didn't seem to care, as he began to slowly pump, in and out, one large hand palming a breast while his fingers teased her nipple, the other entwined in her hair, which fanned out on the pillow behind her.

"Calli," he groaned as she gasped at all of the new sensations that filled her, her every thought and response now wrapped up in him.

He filled her in more ways than one — yes, physically, but also in all of her senses, all of her thoughts, all of her emotions.

As he drove into her and made her feel as though she was being utterly possessed by him, she realized that one time with him was not going to solve everything and satisfy her for the rest of her life.

For she was always going to want this — with him — for as long as she could breathe.

The thought caused everything within her to quicken — her breath, her pulse, her nearness to completion.

"Jonathan," she groaned, clutching him before the waves began to wash over her once more and her world came apart.

Jonathan responded to her release with a shout, and just as the wave began to ebb, he pulled out of her and spent on the bedsheets beside her.

He rolled over onto the other side of her, wrapping an arm around her and drawing her near.

"Calli," he whispered in her ear, "are you all right?"

"That was indescribable," she said, not answering his question, knowing that she would never be all right again, not when she knew what she knew now, of what it was like to be with him, and yet also what was awaiting them in the future.

"It was," he agreed, lying back on the pillow with one arm over his forehead.

"Is it always like that?" she asked in wonder, and he chuckled slightly.

"I'm not much of a rake myself," he said, his fingers playing with her hair in a manner that made her close her eyes and relax into him, "but I can say with all assurance that from what I know, it is almost never like that."

Calli smiled in satisfaction as she snuggled into his side.

"I'm glad to hear it."

He looked over at her, studying her, his lips still curled in a slight smile.

"Who are you, Calliope Donahue?" he asked, "and just how have you bewitched me so?"

Calli froze, staring up at the cherubs dancing on the ceiling, likely judging her, which they had every right to, as she sighed. Calliope Donahue. A non-existent woman.

At least he knew her first name, and he called her by it so she didn't feel like as much of a fraud as she would otherwise.

"What do you want to know?" she asked, searching her mind now desperately for the story she had previously told him, trying to remember what she had shared.

"You told me that you are from a family of merchants," he gently prodded, and she nodded gratefully.

"Yes, of course," she said, deciding to tell him as much of

the truth as she could. "My eldest brother has always been more like a father to the rest of us. Except that he... well he's not really my brother."

"No?"

She could tell Jonathan was attempting nonchalance, although his voice held a slight edge that Calli could only guess was distrust.

"My brother — my true, blood brother — and I were orphaned as children. My eldest brother took us in, gave us a home, supported us," she said. "I have another brother and sister who similarly became part of the family. We are all quite close."

"I see," Jonathan said, lacing his hands behind his head as he stared upward as well. "How did you become a governess?"

"I suppose you could say the profession caught me unawares," she said, attempting levity, which seemed to work as Jonathan simply chuckled. "And you?" Calli asked, desperate to turn the conversation, wondering if Jonathan might be more vulnerable now that the two of them had been together.

Jonathan didn't say anything for a moment, lifting her hand, running a finger over her palm and each individual digit as though he could read all of the secrets within her through them.

Finally, he spoke, his eyes still upon her. "One would think that, as a duke, I could have all I ever want."

Calli said nothing, hoping her silence would urge him on.

"But the truth is, it is difficult to know exactly what one wants. And even when one thinks he is getting it, it turns out that it has nothing to do with him, but only one's title."

"What do you mean?" she asked softly and he paused again. For a moment, Calli was worried she had taken a step too far.

"I became a duke very young. Probably far too young. I wasn't ready. Hadn't learned enough from my father. I thought I knew everything."

He laughed, the bitterness evident.

"I was wrong. Everyone wanted to be my friend, my advisor. I trusted the wrong people, did what they said. I lost so much."

He twined his fingers in between hers.

"Money?"

"Money, yes. Lots of it. On bad investments, gambling, horses."

"I thought you didn't gamble."

"Not anymore. I used to think that I could beat the system, that I would always come out ahead. That I knew better, was smarter. I wasn't."

Calli flipped over on her stomach so that she could better see his face.

"But the worst of it was that I lost friends. People who I now realize that I could trust, I pushed away with my intensity to prove myself, prove I was right, even when they were telling me to take a step back."

"What about the rest of your family?"

"My mother did everything she could to change my ways, but I refused to listen. Eventually she couldn't watch it anymore and left for Bath. She never had much interest in me beyond my usefulness. I am the Duke of Hargreave to her, not... Jonathan. My sister was always too involved in herself — as you might have realized. She left her children in my safekeeping so that she wouldn't feel guilty about leaving them for her new life, as she knew I would care for them."

"Do you mean financially?"

He nodded. "They will want for nothing."

Except all they wanted was his love. Not that Calli was

going to voice that aloud. That was for Jonathan to discover himself.

"But you found your way back, did you not?"

"For the most part, yes. I learned who to trust, made much wiser investments, and have earned back far more than I ever had at the time."

Calli sensed there was something he wasn't saying and debated whether or not she should push. As she looked at him, however, she could sense the unease lurking behind his eyes, and wondered if this was something he needed to get out.

"What else did you lose?"

His eyes flew up to meet hers. "What do you mean?"

"There seems to be something else… something that's bothering you."

"I lost my sense of trust," he said, the words just over a whisper as he dropped his gaze to the covering on the bed. "I was to be married."

"Oh," Calli said softly, annoyed by how the news made her heart skip. "It obviously didn't go forward?"

He shook his head slowly. "The woman… I thought I loved her. She was everything I could ever want in a wife. She was beautiful. Elegant. Appreciated the ways of the nobility. Seemed to understand my every want and need."

"But?"

"But I was being played. She was a young widow, but unbeknownst to me, was the mistress of one of my advisors. He told her everything she needed to know, and together they came up with a scheme that would see me marry her and then together they would slowly divest me of my riches."

"Oh, Jonathan."

"I caught them together. In one of the bedrooms of Wyndmere at a house party I was hosting."

Calli gasped, unable to imagine such a thing. "What did you do?"

"Told them to get out of my house. It wasn't until later that Davenport came to see me and told me the entire story. His father was close with the man. It was that day that we became friends."

"My goodness," Calli murmured, looking down at her fingers as she picked at the threads of the coverlet.

He brought a hand underneath her chin, tilted her head up to look at him. "I have to thank you."

"For what?"

"For teaching me how to trust again." He managed a slight, tremulous smile.

And Calli's heart broke.

CHAPTER 18

Jonathan didn't hear his man of business enter his office the next day.

When he looked up to find him sitting there on the other side of the desk in front of him, he nearly jumped out of his chair.

"Shepherd! What are you doing here?"

"Your butler announced me. I am here to follow up on details of the land acquisition."

"Ah, right," Jonathan said, nodding his head, feeling the fool.

"Is everything all right, Your Grace?"

"Of course, never better. Why do you ask?"

"Well..." Shepherd looked from one side to the other as though to make sure no one could hear him despite the fact they were alone. "You were humming."

"I was not."

"You were," the man insisted, and Jonathan knew that he had to believe him, for Shepherd never, ever joked. "I have never heard you hum before."

"No, I don't suppose you would have," Jonathan said, snapping his jaw shut, determined not to let it happened again. He knew exactly what he had been humming — the same song that Calli sung to herself when she didn't know he was listening.

He had to hide his smile as he thought back to the morning. She had fallen asleep in his bed, and he had to gently wake her up and re-dress her before he sent her on her way, wishing he could let her stay and treat her to a morning she was deserving of, one with warm chocolate and fresh biscuits, as she lay in his bed.

He pictured her as she would look with the rising sun streaming in around her, her long curls strewn out around her head. What a sight she would be.

"Your Grace?"

His man of business brought him back to the present.

"Yes, Shepherd, what was that?"

"I said the sale has gone through and you are the new owner of the land that was previously adjacent to your estate."

"Excellent," Jonathan said. "Will you see to all of the business in order to inform the tenants of the new owner?"

"Of course, Your Grace," Shepherd said with a nod before they proceeded to go over the ledgers that Shepherd presented.

"Shepherd," Jonathan said just as the man was about to leave.

"Yes, Your Grace?"

"We have talked before about the fact that I should soon take a wife."

"We have, Your Grace," Shepherd said, hesitating slightly. "I know it is not my place to offer an opinion, but some of the houses that we oversee, well, it would be helpful to have a woman worry about many of the household issues instead.

And then there are the children to consider. If you didn't have to be the one considering governesses and things…"

The governess. Exactly what was on his mind.

"How much scandal do you think it would cause if I were to marry a woman from outside of the nobility?"

Shepherd's eyes rounded, but he knew better than to offer much commentary. "I—I couldn't say, Your Grace, not being from the nobility myself."

"Right. Perhaps I better ask Davenport. I am due to meet with him shortly. Good day, Shepherd, and thank you."

"Your Grace," Shepherd said with a nod, and when he was halfway out the door, he turned around and looked at Jonathan. "One more thing."

"Yes?"

"There are a pair of feet beneath your curtains."

Jonathan heard the giggle before he turned to look, and he let out a sigh.

"Come out, Mary."

She scrambled out of the curtains, coming to stand in front of his desk with an eager smile.

"Are you going to marry Miss Donahue?"

Jonathan fixed what he hoped was a stern look on his face. "Now, Mary, I never said such a thing, you know that."

"But you said you were going to marry… and someone outside of the nobility. It *must* be Miss Donahue."

"I was simply asking a question about… something I was pondering," he said, willing the child to stay silent about what she had so proudly discovered. "Now, speaking of Miss Donahue, where is she?"

"Looking for me, undoubtedly. I hid the one place she wouldn't dare look."

"Go find her, or I shall have to return you to her myself, which you most assuredly do not want."

The child heaved a long-suffering sigh. "Very well."

Jonathan shook his head as Mary skipped out of the room. He honestly didn't think there was anything Calli or any other governess could ever do to tame these children. They had minds of their own. And the truth was? He was coming to appreciate them. Most certainly far more than he ever thought he would.

He called for his hat and cloak and soon found himself within the hallowed grounds of White's. He was not a frequent visitor — not as his father had been — but he far preferred the establishment to those that were of lesser repute. At least, at White's, one knew what to expect. Who to expect. Even if that company was not always welcome.

"Hargreave, is that a smile I see on your face?"

Jonathan looked up to find Davenport awaiting him at a table, a decanter and two glasses in front of him.

"Davenport, I see you've started without me."

"Well, I knew you weren't likely to imbibe much anyway, so I might as well enjoy."

Jonathan nodded in agreement, even as he noted Davenport tilting his head to the side as he studied him.

"Something is different about you," Davenport finally said.

"Whatever do you mean?"

"I'm not sure," Davenport mused. "At first I thought it was something you changed in your appearance, but the more I look at you, the more I wonder…"

"What?" Jonathan said, becoming annoyed now.

"You know," Davenport put a finger on his lips, tapping it against them, "I think you actually look happy."

"When have I not been happy?" Jonathan asked, to which Davenport let out a bark of laughter, although he quickly sobered at Jonathan's glare, belatedly attempting to cover his levity with a cough and a sip of his drink.

"Well, you are usually a bit more… severe."

"Severe?"

"Imposing."

"I see."

"No insult intended, Hargreave. Just an observation. But tell me… has anything changed?"

"Well…" Jonathan hedged. He had wanted to ask Davenport his opinion but now was unsure whether or not his friend would simply ridicule him. Finally he sighed, his need to discuss the matter winning out over how Davenport might react. "I am thinking of getting married."

Davenport eyed him over the rim of his glass. "Getting married as in holding a ball to determine whether there might be a young woman who would suit, or getting married as in actually having a woman in mind with whom you would tie yourself for the rest of your life?"

"The latter."

Davenport paused, studying Jonathan for a moment.

"Good God, man!" He said, slamming down his now-empty cup. "You are serious."

"I am."

"Who is she?"

Jonathan hesitated. "I'm not entirely comfortable in saying as of yet, for I have not actually discussed such a thing with the woman."

"What woman wouldn't marry you?" Davenport asked with a snort. "She would be a fool to say no to a powerful man such as yourself."

"That's just the thing, Davenport," Jonathan said, his own wonder at the entire situation growing. "I think she is the one woman who actually sees me for who I am and not what my title is."

Davenport leaned forward on his elbows, staring at Jonathan with more intensity than he ever typically held.

"Go on."

"There's not much more to say," he said with a shrug. "She just seems to understand me in a way that not many do. Even puts up with my... gruffness."

Davenport laughed at that. "Not many do."

"There is just one problem," Jonathan said, with a slight grimace. "She is not from the nobility. Not even close. I don't even know who her parents are. She was orphaned at a young age."

Davenport sat back in his chair, crossing his arms over his chest. "Well, this is interesting."

"How much of a scandal do you think it would cause?"

"It would be the talk of the *ton* for a time, that is for certain," Davenport said, scratching his chin, "although likely only until the next great scandal came along. You know how they all are."

"Do I ever," Jonathan muttered.

"I suppose," Davenport said, tapping his glass against the table, "You have to decide what is worth more — spending your life with a woman of your own choosing, or with one who the *ton* would approve of?"

Jonathan nodded. "I know I do not spend a great deal of time in the public eye, but there are times when I have to play host or attend dinner parties for one reason or another. I would not want my wife to be ridiculed."

"No," Davenport said, although he seemed in agreement, "but for how long would they ridicule a duchess until they realized it was not in their best interests? If the woman is strong enough — and I would guess she is, if she is willing to go up against you — then I am sure she would be well prepared to take on whatever comes her way."

Lightness began to fill Jonathan's chest.

"You're right," he said, already rising without having taken a sip of the drink in front of him.

"Leaving so soon?" Davenport asked, a twinkle in his eye, and Jonathan nodded.

"Yes, I have… business to attend to."

"Give Miss Donahue my best."

"I wi—" Jonathan whirled around, his mouth open. "How did you know?"

Davenport laughed with a shrug. "Lucky guess, I suppose. Best wishes, Hargreave."

Jonathan shocked Davenport by answering his wide grin with one of his own, and then he was out the door, off to win over his governess.

* * *

"Miss Donahue! Miss Donahue, it's your turn to hide!"

Calli ran across the green to find a place behind one of the benches, knowing she was not terribly well hidden but at least it gave her the ability to keep an eye on the children. She didn't particularly enjoy playing hide-and-seek with Mary and Matthew for they were far too cunning and clever and she didn't quite trust them, but she had run out of ideas to keep them entertained.

"Calli."

Calli turned quickly to find Xander in the bush behind her and she toppled backwards. When she pushed herself back into a crouching position rather ungracefully, she glared at him.

"Why must you continue to frighten me?" she hissed. "Now is not the time. The children will be here in moments."

"I know. I will be quick. Arie wants to see you. Tonight."

"I can't."

"You must."

"I *can't*. I am almost done with the painting. I need just a couple more nights."

"You should have been done days ago."

Calli cast her brother a withering glare. "I have been occupied."

"There she is!" Calli heard Mary exclaim, and she motioned Xander away.

"I'll be back for you at midnight," he said as he slunk backward. "Be waiting by the servants' entrance. Bring the statue."

Then he slipped away before she could respond. She was still wearing her frown when Mary found her, and she forced a smile upon her face.

She had a lot to decide before she met with Arie tonight. She had thought she could do this, what her family expected of her, but after last night with Jonathan... her doubts grew as her affection for him increased. She had to decide what she wanted — approval from her family, or to earn Jonathan's trust. She knew he had provided her with a great gift, and she couldn't seem to find it within her to squander it.

But how was she to make her family understand?

* * *

JONATHAN FELT all eyes on him once more during dinner.

He knew it was likely because he couldn't stop smiling. He had even found himself humming again at one point in time, until Matthew had pointed it out.

Tonight. Tonight was the night. He was going to ask Calli to be his wife. He had a fine plan. It would just be the two of them. He would send his valet to bed early, would prepare the room himself. He wouldn't tell anyone until afterward. He looked at Mary and Matthew, who seemed perplexed now, but who, he knew, would be so pleased when they shared the news with them.

He couldn't remember ever acting so impulsively — at least, since he had learned his lesson — but it felt better than he ever could have imagined.

"Why did you invite us to dinner, Uncle?" Mary asked, never one to mince words, and Jonathan couldn't help but smile.

"Did you not enjoy dinner together when we were at Wyndmere?"

"Yes, but you said we would only eat together there."

"Well, I find myself away from Parliament tonight, so I thought we could dine together."

"That is very thoughtful of your uncle, Mary, is it not?" Calli asked with a pointed look at her charge, who nodded slowly.

"Yes. It is odd though."

"Mary."

"Sorry, Miss Donahue."

"Apologize to your uncle."

"Sorry, Uncle."

"Nothing to worry about." He took a bite of the duck, prepared perfectly by the cook who had been with him for years. "Miss Donahue, you seem quiet tonight."

Calli's dark head snapped up. "I do?"

"You do," he said, although he softened his words with a smile.

She shrugged. "Just tired, I suppose."

"Not again," he said, curling his mouth into a wicked grin as he recalled — in detail — just exactly what had kept her up all night. She flushed as she took a sip of her wine.

"I shall be fine with a good sleep tonight," she said with determination as she set the glass back down.

Not if he had anything to do about it.

He tried not to overtly watch her as they were served one course after another, finishing with chocolate cake that Calli refused but Jonathan relished, and he caught her eye as he took a bite, licking the last bit of icing from his lip. Calli looked away, but he could tell from the rise of her breast and the pulse that beat within her neck that she was not as unaffected as one might think.

She took the children to bed shortly after dinner, and Jonathan found it difficult to keep himself occupied and not think of what was to come in the hour or so that followed. He prepared his bedchamber with candles, stoking the fire continually to ensure it was warm enough for her, and even brought in a bouquet of red and yellow flowers he had spied on the hall table, as foolish as he felt in doing so.

But he wanted everything to be right.

He walked over to the chest of drawers in the corner, pulling out the middle drawer, feeling around beneath the garments within until he found the hard box he was looking for.

He snapped open the lid, staring at, for the first time in many years, the ring his grandmother had worn. He had given it to another, once, and had been fortunate enough to have it returned — at least, after he had threatened *complete* ruination.

Jonathan intended that the next time he gave it away, it would stay on the finger of the woman for the rest of her life.

Now all she had to do was agree.

Finally, the hour was sufficient for him to go to her. Secretly, he had been hoping that she would return to his bedroom herself, but he could understand her hesitancy in doing so.

He took a breath before knocking lightly on her door, waiting with great anticipation for her face to peek through.

But there was no response.

He slowly turned the knob and pushed open the door,

only to find the room void of any presence, the fire even down to embers in the hearth.

Calli wasn't here — so just where had she gone?

CHAPTER 19

"Arie, I really don't have time to be here. I told Xander that."

"So he related to me. But Calli, *I* don't have time to wait any longer either. My buyer is running out of patience. This entire affair should have been dealt with days ago."

"Replicating a master's work is not as simple as you might think."

Arie fixed a benevolent smile on her, one that she hated, for it made her feel like a young child.

"That is not what you said when you assured me weeks ago that you could take this on. Something has changed, Calli. Best you start telling me just what that is."

Calli looked around the room for sympathy from her other siblings. But Diana, of course, stood beside Arie, his ever-faithful general, while even Xander seemed to be awaiting her response. Damien looked pained, as he always did whenever he could sense controversy within the family.

"You must understand, Arie, that I am working with the children all day and then painting all night. It is exhausting."

"Right," Arie said, standing from the chair that Calli knew

he considered his throne of sorts before he walked toward her. He leaned over her chair, holding her captive between his arms as he stared her down. "So none of those nocturnal hours are spent... otherwise?"

His eyes flashed and, in that moment, Calli knew. He was aware of her relationship with Jonathan. How much he knew, she had no idea, but however much it was, it was enough.

She must act ignorant. She gasped aloud indignantly. "How dare you?"

"How dare I what? Find out? I have eyes and ears everywhere. Even in a duke's castle."

Calli cast a look over at Xander, who wouldn't meet her eye. She gritted her teeth, for she was well aware where those 'eyes and ears' usually came from — pretty maids or serving girls that Xander charmed.

"There is nothing to discover. The duke and I have become... friends, yes, but nothing more. Which is a good thing, for then he has little cause to suspect me."

"And you still feel that you can betray your... *friend*?"

Arie leaned back now, releasing her, and Calli took a breath of the air that seemed to return once he gave her space.

"If I am to be honest, I will tell you that I do feel some guilt at the fact that I am deceiving him, yes," Calli said, determined to hold true to the promise she had made to herself. She was going to make this right. She was going to make *all* of this right. She just wasn't sure how. Not yet. "He took me into his home, gave me a position on his staff. It just feels... *wrong* to do this to him."

As Diana's eyes widened, Arie snorted in disgust.

"He is a duke, Calli. It will make no difference to him whether or not one painting goes missing. For him it is equivalent to anyone else losing a pound note. He likely won't even be the wiser."

Except Calli would know. And she knew far better — yes, it may be inconsequential to Jonathan in terms of wealth, but if he were to discover her deception, it would change everything. He would not only never want to see her again, but he might be forever changed.

She swallowed, standing as she faced Arie, determined not to let him intimidate her.

"I would know, Arie."

He scoffed at her. "You never were quite one of us."

The words struck her painfully deep within, far more than she could ever allow him to know, causing her to shake so hard she had to grip her hands into fists at her side to keep him from seeing their trembling. Diana's gaze flicked down, perceptive as always.

"Arie," Xander said, unfurling his long frame from where he sat astride a hard-backed chair. "That's not fair. Calli has never been anything but loyal to all of us."

"Until now, apparently."

Xander looked uncertainly from Arie to Calli, as though unsure of just where his loyalty should lie. That hurt nearly as much as Arie's words for, if anything, she thought she would always have the support of the brother who had been there since the day she was born.

"I'll not go through with it — not anymore," she said, holding her head high, and Arie shocked her when he simply laughed.

"You don't have a choice."

"I do."

"No," Arie said, shaking his head. "You don't. For I am going to steal that painting — whether you agree or not. And if I steal the painting without your help, I will be sure to inform your beloved Jonathan just what role you played in it all."

"You wouldn't," Calli ground out. "That would only implicate yourself."

"I have my ways to ensure that I am never found out," Arie said smugly. "As for you, however…. Listen, Calli, at least this way, you have a chance that he might never find out the truth."

"But *I* shall always know it," she all but whispered, and Arie shrugged, apparently not caring.

"Now, I hear you have acquired a statue for me."

Calli shook her head. "You heard wrong."

She couldn't do it. She had left the statue back at Jonathan's house. Somehow, she was going to return it to the baron. She didn't know how yet, but she would.

Arie looked from Calli to Xander. "Well, well. One of you is lying to me. Just which one of you is it?"

Calli looked to Xander, hoping he understood her plea not to give away her secrets.

Her brother stared at her, fighting a war within himself, until finally he turned to Arie,

"I must have been mistaken," he murmured, to which Arie waved him away with a hand.

"Fine, then. Keep your statue," he said, but his eye twitched as he stared at Calli. "But the painting is mine. Send word when we can come and switch them out. No longer than two days' time, Calli. Do you understand me?"

She nodded mutely. "Understood," she whispered.

Xander didn't say much on the return journey, but as he left her near the servants' entrance of Jonathan's house, he stopped her before she left the carriage, grabbing her wrist. "I'm sorry, Calli," he said, his words low. "But there's nothing else we can do. You agreed to this."

"I know," she said miserably before she bid him goodnight and let herself into the house.

She was hardly aware of her surroundings as she walked up to her room, wishing now only for the comfort of her bed. She might as well enjoy it while she could.

Which is why she nearly stumbled over the pair of feet hanging off her bed. She caught herself in time, looking up to find herself staring at Jonathan — and her painting spread out in front of him.

* * *

Jonathan had heard her come in. Walk down the hall. He waited for her, sitting on her bed. The longer he had waited as he watched his lone candle burn low, the more his ire had grown, until he was nearly shaking with it.

He tried to tell himself that he should be patient. That he should give her a chance to explain. But instead, it seemed all his mind was capable of doing was imagining all of the reasons that a near-perfect copy of his painting was underneath her bed.

"Jonathan."

Her voice was breathless, defensive, and he looked up at her, no longer seeing the woman he had come to know so intimately, the one he had thought he would marry, but instead someone he knew nothing about.

"What is this?"

He threw his hand out before him, hearing the disgust in his voice, even though, had she asked, he would have been forced to admit that it was a masterpiece. For it looked like the very painting he stared at from his study desk each and every day.

"It's... it's a painting."

"It's my painting."

"Yes and no."

"What," he seethed, "is that supposed to mean?"

"It means that it is a copy of your painting, yes, but that I was the one who painted it."

"Why?"

She shrank back from him, bringing a finger to her lips as her eyes darted to the second doorway.

"Please be quiet, or you will wake the children."

"You mean the very children that you have left for your late-night wanderings?" He raised an eyebrow. "Where have you been?"

She took a step back into the room, holding her hands out in front of her, palms up, as though she was quieting him. "Perhaps we should take a moment and calm down."

"Pardon me?" The words were clipped, and from the way her eyes flicked back and forth, he knew he was scaring her, but he didn't care at the moment.

"I just think… that, well, perhaps if we sat down, had a reasonable conversation, we could figure this out. You seem very… angry right now."

"I seem angry."

"Yes."

She deliberately didn't meet his gaze, instead taking slow and steady paces across the room before unfastening her cloak and hanging it on the hook. Jonathan had stood from the bed, staring down at the painting feeling vaguely that it was insulting him. Calli took a seat next to it, patting the bed beside her.

"Sit, please?"

"No, thank you. Why don't you tell me where you have been and what this painting is for before I pack it all up for you?"

"Very well," she said, looking down at her intertwined fingers. "I love the painting in your office. I truly do. I wanted to have a copy of it for myself. I thought it would be good practice for me to see how close I could come to replicating it."

"It looks identical. Just missing a few details."

"Thank you?" she said, looking up at him with some hesitation.

"Tell me this, Calli," he said, crouching down and staring at her so that she had no choice but to look at him. "Were you going to try to sell it? Make some money off it?"

"No."

"Where were you going to put it?"

He looked around the room, holding his hands up.

"I don't know. I wasn't sure how long I would be here, I suppose."

"And just where," he stood and placed his hands on his hips, "did you think you would be going?"

She shrugged, looking small and unsure, and he began to somewhat regret the tone he had taken with her.

"I don't know, Jonathan," she said softly. "I figured that, someday, you would marry, or court a young woman, and I wouldn't be able to stay any longer."

"Why would you think that?" he asked gruffly, although he could understand why she would assume she would have to leave. He knew he would never be able to see her with another.

"The night we met, you were hosting an event to try to find a wife, were you not?" she asked, her eyes wide and glossy as she looked at him.

"How did you know that?"

"The children told me."

"I see," he said, clasping his hands behind his back as he began to pace the room. "Would you care to tell me where you were tonight?"

"I had to go check in on my family."

"The sick relative again?"

"Yes."

"And?"

"He is doing much better."

"If you need time to go see family, you know you just need to ask me," Jonathan said, wondering why she wouldn't feel she was able to.

"I know, but I am aware that I am only provided my one day a week. I wouldn't want to ask you for any more on account of you—we…" she looked away, apparently not able to properly describe what they were to each other.

"Calli," he said, attempting to soften his words, "I wouldn't say no to you, no matter what our relationship. I hope you would know that I am rather benevolent with my staff."

"I wasn't sure," she said softly.

Jonathan sighed, placing his hands behind his back. She had provided reasonable explanations for the painting, for her whereabouts, and yet, he had the sense that all was not as it seemed. He had trusted before and was made the fool, and he was not about to allow that to happen again. He thought back to how excited he had been earlier this evening, and he wished that he hadn't allowed anyone else to see it, not even Davenport. For there was no way that he could, at least at the moment, ask anything further of Calli than the relationship they already had. Not until he was sure, until he knew who she was and where she came from, until he could completely trust her.

"Since you seem so close to your family, I was wondering…"

"Yes?"

"Perhaps the children and I could meet them sometime. We could arrange a trip to Gunter's or something of the sort."

"To Gunter's? With my family?" she repeated him, her eyes widening and her mouth rounding as though she could never imagine the thought.

"Would that be an issue?"

"Yes. No. I—"

"In two days' time."

"I shall ask."

"See that you do," he said, striding to the door, taking one last look back at Calli and then the painting. "Goodnight, Calli."

"Goodnight, Jonathan."

CHAPTER 20

She should have just told him the truth.

But if she had, she didn't think he would ever forgive her. And why, by all that was holy, did he want to meet her family?

While Calli hoped her explanations that night had been reasonable, she was aware that she had broken some degree of trust between them — trust that she knew Jonathan didn't take lightly. For the past two days, he had kept distance between them, not coming to her at night, and all but ignoring her during the day. They did not eat dinner together as he was back in Parliament, and Calli found herself having to explain to the children their uncle's seemingly sudden abandonment.

"He has been busy," she said the following morning. "But he promised we would go to Gunter's today."

"He did?" Mary asked, her eyes brightening. "It has been some time since I have been to Gunter's."

"I have never been."

They stared at her with mouths agape.

"You haven't?"

"No," she laughed at their shock. "I haven't."

She had sent a message to her family, addressing it to Xander. She asked if he and Damien would come, and hoped that Arie and Diana would not accompany them. Arie would raise all of Jonathan's suspicions, while one never knew just what Diana was going to say. She would also certainly report everything back to Arie.

This morning, a cryptic note had arrived for her at the servants' entrance — one the butler passed to her with as much wariness as Jonathan held for her.

It read, *see you at Gunter's.*

Thankfully, Calli recognized Xander's handwriting, but she had no idea just who would be accompanying him.

They would find out soon. Three hours later, she and the children were descending the staircase to meet Jonathan. She lifted her gaze to his with some trepidation, but his face was devoid of any emotion or sign of what he was thinking. She sighed.

"Come, children," she said, leading them out to the waiting carriage, Jonathan following.

The carriage ride was filled with the children's chattering, both of them excited for the awaiting treat. Calli sat across from Jonathan, looking out the window as she tried to evade his probing stare.

"Is there anything amiss, Miss Donahue?" he asked, raising his eyebrows.

"No," she said, forcing a smile. "Nothing at all."

"Who from your family shall be joining us?"

"I am not entirely sure," she said truthfully. They disembarked at Gunter's, and Calli breathed in relief that it wasn't crowded today, that at least there would not be many witnesses to whatever was going to occur here.

They descended from the carriage to find Xander — and Arie, who smiled at her with such slickness that Calli nearly went rigid. As it was, Matthew had to poke her to take another step into the small shop.

"Calli," Arie greeted her as the two imposing men walked over toward them. "How good for you to invite us."

"Your Grace, may I please introduce my brothers, Xander and Arie H—Donahue?" She fixed a gaze on them, pleading for them to go along, but she had nothing to fear. They were both well versed in the art of deception.

"A pleasure to meet you, Your Grace," Arie said with a graceful bow. "And these must be the two amazing children our Calli has told us all about."

Mary giggled while Matthew looked wary, and Calli was impressed that he could already see through her brother's facade.

"Tell me, how fares your ailing—uncle, was it?" Jonathan asked warmly, and fortunately the only thing to skip a beat was Calli's heart.

"Doing much better," Arie said smoothly. "Much better indeed. We so appreciate Calli's diligence to ensure that he is well."

"Of course you do," Jonathan said. "Why don't I buy us all some ice and we can continue this conversation?"

"We can pay for our own," Arie said, straightening, and Calli hoped he would not allow his arrogance to ruin everything.

"I invited you here," Jonathan said, the ducal authority in his voice barring any argument. "I will pay."

Arie held his head high as he eyed Jonathan, the two of them in some kind of masculine standoff, and Calli rolled her eyes as she stepped up between them to try to ease the tension.

"Thank you so much, Your Grace," she said. "Shall we choose our flavours?"

Fortunately, the children broke much of the strains of

unease with their exuberance, and soon enough they were all sitting around a table in a corner of the shop, licking their ices while they stared at one another. Calli would have found it comical was she not the one who was in the middle of it all.

"Tell me more about what you do," Jonathan said to her brothers. "Calli tells me that you are in trade?"

"We are," Arie said, a slow smile spreading across his face at Calli's description of how they made their living. "We specialize in priceless items."

"Such as?"

"Artifacts. Paintings. Items that usually go to auction. We find specialized buyers for them."

"Sounds like something illicit," Jonathan said, lowering his ice as he considered Arie, and Arie's eyes darkened, causing Calli's pulse to quicken. When Arie became angry, one did not want to be in his way.

"I assure you that all who we work with are deserving of what they receive," Arie said, his words clipped, and Calli and Xander exchanged a look.

"Jon—His Grace has made investments in trade himself," Calli added, trying to turn the direction of the conversation, "so he is interested in the work of others."

"A duke who sullies his hands in trade?" Arie said, raising his eyebrows. "How intriguing."

"Intriguing, or intelligent?" Jonathan shot back, and Calli sighed inwardly. This had been the worst idea anyone had ever had. Why hadn't she tried harder to avoid it? "I have made far more through my investments than I ever have through my entailments. I am able to properly provide for others because of it."

"Provide for people such as my sister?" Arie said, leaning forward now. "For I assure you that I can do a fine enough job of that myself."

"Then just why did she find employment as my

governess?" Jonathan asked, obviously quite interested now in the answer to the question, and Calli saw the flicker of annoyance in Arie's eyes when he realized his misstep.

"I believe I can answer that," Calli said, leaning forward from where she sat next to the children. "It is important to me to provide for myself, to have a purpose in life."

Which was true.

"I see," Jonathan said, although he eyed her with some distrust that caused an unease deep within her belly to grow. "Although I recall how you developed your interest in painting. I'm surprised that you were so in awe by my gallery if you are usually surrounded by works that your brother trades in."

"I… don't often have a chance to see what he is working with," Calli murmured as she eyed her ice, which moments ago she had considered absolutely delicious, but which now she was slowly losing her appetite for. She just wanted to have this over with, to get out of here and move on, keeping both parts of her life separate.

Until one would be lost to her forever.

"Tell us more about your gallery, Your Grace," Xander said, a greedy flash in his eyes, while Arie sat back, allowing their brother to do the talking, although Calli was well aware he was just as interested.

"It's simply a gallery of his favorite works," Calli murmured, "a place for himself."

"Any painters we might know?" Xander asked.

"A few," Jonathan answered, but cleared his throat and said no more, his own intuition obviously picking up on the fact that this was not something he should be speaking about — at least, not with this family.

"Uncle has tons and tons of paintings on the wall," Matthew added now, trying to be helpful, but Calli wished he would stop. "It's creepy how all the people in them look down on you. I don't even know how they all got up there, they are so high!"

"I can imagine," Arie said with a grin for the boy.

"Calli showed you her paintings?" Xander asked now, apparently belatedly realizing what had first turned the conversation this way.

"I... stumbled in on one of her paintings," Jonathan said, sending a look her way. "She's quite talented."

"That she is," Xander said proudly.

"She tells me that she is only blood-related to one of you, is that correct?" Jonathan asked, looking at Xander, obviously realizing which one of them it was.

"Yes," Arie said, the glint back in his eyes, "but we have been family for so long that it doesn't really matter."

"And just how did that come to be?" Jonathan asked, and Calli looked between him and Arie, wondering just why he would care so much about her background. She had told him everything he should need to know.

"Calli and Xander were on the streets. Alone." Arie leaned forward again, his ice discarded beside him. "I provided them with a home. Purpose. Family. We built ourselves up from nothing."

"Here in London?" Jonathan persisted, not cowed by the force of Arie's words.

"Yes, here in London," Arie said.

"Is that where you are from?"

Arie had always maintained just a touch of accent, while his Greek complexion always caused confusion for those who had not travelled much outside of England.

"No," Arie said. "I am not."

And it was obvious he would say no more.

"Well, this has been... enlightening," Jonathan said, beginning to rise, Calli quickly following suit.

Arie was well-versed in the etiquette of the noble class,

but he maintained his seated posture for a moment longer, as though to purposefully irk Jonathan.

"Thank you for the ices," Xander said, before dipping into a bow in front of the children, who giggled at him. Xander had always had a way with the young ones. "My lord, my lady." Belatedly he turned. "Your Grace. And Calli, I hope to see you again very soon, sister."

"Of course," she said.

"We shall be away for a couple of days," Jonathan said, and Calli turned to him with some surprise. "My mother has just returned from Bath, and we will go to the country to visit her for the weekend while Parliament is in recess before we return to London."

"Oh, dear," Mary said, her face suddenly frozen in an unnamed fear, "not Grandmother."

"She's not that bad," Jonathan said with a sigh, but as he ran a hand through his hair, Calli had the impression that he was in agreement with the children.

"Calli, before we go, might we talk to you for a moment—alone?" Arie asked, and Calli hesitated before Jonathan gave her a small nod.

They bid their final farewells to Jonathan and the children before they walked outside, down the street a way so that they would be out of earshot if Jonathan came outdoors.

"Seems like you've got yourself into a nice, comfortable family position with the duke and the children, eh?" Arie said, eyeing her, and Calli placed a hand over her chest in defense as she looked up at him.

"What are you talking about?"

"I'm no fool," Arie bit out. "There is something between you and the nob. If you've gotten closer to him to further our work, that is all well and good, but if you have feelings for him, Calli…"

"There is nothing between us," she lied, hoping to convince Arie.

Arie roved his eyes over her face, assessing her.

"Good. Because you need to be thinking with your head. I've always taught you that."

She nodded.

"But the duke obviously has some designs on you. Why else would he invite your family for ices?"

"I—" Her mind went blank. "I don't know."

"Exactly."

He and Xander exchanged a look.

"Here's what's going to happen," Arie said, holding up a finger. "Make your excuses, but do not go with the duke and the children to the country. Remain in London. We will come and switch out the painting and you will be gone, along with the original, before he returns."

Panic began to swirl within Calli's stomach, before it began to claw its way up her throat. If she did what Arie said... she would never see Jonathan again.

"But what kind of excuse would I make?"

"Tell him that you are feeling ill, too ill for the trip. Then when he is gone, just leave a note saying that you had to return to your family or something of the like. Your name is not your name, so he will have no idea where to look for you — not that he is likely to do so."

"Why — because I am so expendable?"

Arie looked at her with pity.

"You have many fine qualities, Calli. You are beautiful, you are intelligent, and you have obviously been good with his children. But there are more of you out there. He is a duke. It will not be hard to find someone to replace you."

Calli had no idea whether he meant as his governess or in his heart, but somehow she had the feeling that it wouldn't have mattered — Arie's opinion would have been the same.

"I—" She felt sick, but she squared her shoulders as she looked up at them both. "I can't do this."

"You said that before," Arie said, his mouth twisting into what she knew was supposed to be a smile but was, in fact, anything but, "and I told you what would happen if you didn't go through with it. Do it my way, he never needs to know the truth about you. Force us to go your way, and I will end up with the painting while he will forever know your duplicity. Which do you prefer?"

"I'm your sister, Arie," she pleaded, but that only served to harden his resolve.

"Yes. And as my sister, you should be loyal to me. Not a nob you only just met. We will see you in two days."

Then they were gone, striding down the street, as Xander looked back at her with sympathy. All Calli could do was take a breath, turn around, and pray for a way out of this.

CHAPTER 21

Jonathan hadn't been planning another country trip so soon, but when his mother had requested to see the grandchildren, he had actually decided that perhaps now was as good a time as any to get out of the city. He had enjoyed himself last time, as had the children and Calli.

Calli.

He let out a breath as he stared out his study window and into the night sky. What was he to do with her? He had thought she was everything he had ever wanted, and yet... there was something that was not quite right. Meeting her family had not satisfied him, had instead only raised more questions. Her brother had been less than reassuring, continually challenging him and obviously contemptuous of his title. Which was not at all Jonathan's fault.

He whirled around when he heard a noise at the door to find Calli standing just within.

"Jonathan?" she asked, and he motioned her to take a step inside.

"You are awake late once again."

"I know," she said, her gaze flickering past him to the painting that hung on the wall, the one she had been so enamoured with she had apparently been compelled to paint it herself.

"I'm sorry about my brother," she said, wringing her hands together. "Arie can be… difficult."

Jonathan grunted. "I am still somewhat perplexed as to what brought you to work for me, or how, quite frankly, you first became a governess with your background. Most are from families with much more prestige."

"I know. I…" her eyes flickered around the room before finally landing on him. "That was actually a bit of an accident."

"What do you mean?" he asked, all of his senses suddenly on alert.

"I'm not… I'm not Miss Donahue."

Jonathan's entire body went rigid, the words forming on his tongue of their own accord.

"What are you talking about?"

"I was always here… to see this painting. I had heard of it, and wanted the opportunity to try my hand at it. So I came into your study to see it, and the children were here. You mistook me for the governess, and it sounded like an excellent opportunity, so I went along with it."

Jonathan noted her shaking hands, her pleading eyes, but he couldn't get over the words that had just tumbled from her mouth.

"So this… you… it's all a lie?"

No, it couldn't be. She was fabricating this, now. But why?

"Not entirely," she said, her eyes looking up at him soulfully, but the more she spoke, the more Jonathan's resolve hardened. "I did want to be a governess to Mary and

Matthew. I enjoy being their governess. I appreciate the position in your household. But since we have become…"

"Lovers."

Her eyes flared at the word.

"Yes. I needed to tell you the truth."

"And your brothers, they went along with this little scheme of yours?"

"I told them this is what I wanted to do. They weren't initially pleased, but, well…"

She scratched her head as though she didn't know what else to say, and Jonathan just stared at her, knowing, somehow, that this was not the end of the story. He could see the uneasiness in her eyes.

"What else?"

"What do you mean?"

"What else are you hiding from me?" He advanced upon her, uncaring that he seemed to be frightening her. Good. She deserved it.

"N-nothing."

He towered over her, looking down at her, and she took a step back, setting her jaw determinately, and he had to admire her spirit as much as he hated the reason for it.

"I told you everything. Shared with you things that had happened to me that I never tell anyone. I *trusted* you."

"I know that," she said, lifting her gaze to stare him in the eye. "And I appreciate it. I am aware how hard that was for you."

He snorted, crossing his arms over his chest.

"It is why I am sharing all with you now," she said, holding her arms out to the side as though trying to display how open she was. "I want you to know who I really am. I am Calliope Murphy. My brother is Xander Murphy. We kept our parents' last name. I may not have had much training to be a governess, but I love Mary and Matthew and I am so grateful for the time I have spent with them. And—" she swallowed, and Jonathan watched the bobbing of her throat. Her voice dropped. "I am falling for you."

Jonathan stood there, unmoving.

"Are you going to say anything?" she finally asked, her eyes wide, watery, pleading.

"How am I supposed to know what to believe, when our entire relationship is based on a lie?" he asked, his words hard, but he found that he couldn't allow himself to soften for her, not one inch.

"But it wasn't," she insisted. "Everything I have felt for you, for the children, it has all been true."

"Except that you are not who you say you are. Tell me, are your brothers really your brothers?"

"In every way that I have explained," she said. "Xander is my brother by blood, while Arie took us in when our parents passed."

"And they truly work in artifacts and priceless objects?"

Her eyes shifted to the side. "Yes, in a sense."

"What do you they actually do?"

She lifted her shoulders. "That is not my secret to share. It is theirs."

"So you will not betray their confidence, but you will betray mine?"

"It's not like that," she insisted, but her nostrils flared as she fisted her fingers at her sides. "But you know what? I can only defend myself for so long. If you insist on being so wilfully vengeful, so be it. I don't know how else to prove to you that I mean what I say."

"Don't try to turn this back around on me."

"What do you want from me, Jonathan?"

He breathed in deeply as he stared at her, wishing she wasn't so beautiful, that his pull toward her wasn't so strong, that he didn't want her as badly as he did.

"I want you to never have lied to me. I want you to have respected the trust I placed in you. I want you to have realized that I would never have allowed a fraud to care for my niece and nephew."

"You cannot continue to dwell on the mistakes I've made without looking forward at what could be done."

He looked down at her, his heart at war with his mind. Part of him wanted to reach out and gather her in his arms and tell her that he didn't care what her name was or where she came from, that she was going to be his and he would give her a new name, one that she could hold onto forever.

But that was ludicrous. She would be a duchess, then. His duchess. And he didn't even know who she truly was.

"I need to think about this."

"I understand." She shrank back away from him, and he had never felt more alone.

"I don't think you should come to the country to meet my mother."

She looked down as she hugged her arms around herself. "Very well."

She dropped her arms, turning around and walking to the door. She stood there for a moment, one hand on the doorframe as she looked back at him, every inch the goddess she was, although a very sad one at the moment.

"Goodbye, Jonathan."

As she continued down the hallway, he wondered why it felt like she was saying goodbye forever.

* * *

CALLI STARED MOROSELY at the painting lying on the bed in front of her.

It was finished. It was perfect. And she had never felt so incomplete.

She sank down beside the bed, her head in her hands. Jonathan and children were gone, left for the country. While she remained, alone, just waiting for her brothers to come and complete her betrayal.

She had thought that she was doing the right thing by sharing at least a little bit of her true self with Jonathan. Instead, it had done the opposite, only furthering his deepening distrust in her.

Telling him the first bit of truth had been her attempt to see just whether or not he might ever be accepting of her if it turned out she was not who she said she was.

Whatever she thought might have been a potential match between them was completely gone now. The façade of their moments together had been just that — moments. There would be nothing more, and she had been a fool to ever consider that there could be.

He was a duke, for goodness sake.

She was nothing, no one.

No, that wasn't quite true.

She was a fraud, from a family of thieves.

Now her brothers would be here tonight to steal from Jonathan, to take the painting that would be the final tie to be severed between them. Even if he never found out, she would always know.

Unless…

An idea came to her. One that was rather extreme, and would require her to act quickly. She looked at her painting, then at the packed bags beside it.

She would leave, yes, no matter what happened, for to stay would only lead to her own heartbreak.

But she could make things right.

She had to.

CHAPTER 22

"I don't understand, Uncle, why isn't Miss Donahue with us?"

"She wasn't feeling well."

Jonathan was, perhaps, prolonging the inevitable, but he couldn't bring himself to tell the children that they might have to soon say goodbye to their governess forever.

Especially when they seemed to love her so much.

Her, after so many other governesses had fallen short.

"She seemed quite well to me," Matthew said, crossing his arms over his chest as he stared up at Jonathan with contempt he did not quite understand. "Did you say something mean to her?"

"Pardon me?" Jonathan said, lifting a brow in an expression he hoped would command more respect from his nephew.

"She looked so sad when we saw her this morning. Mary and I thought maybe you said something to make her unhappy."

Jonathan drew in a breath, attempting to find patience. "I told you that she wasn't feeling well. That must have been it."

"Do you love her?"

Jonathan started from his seat across from the children in the carriage. "Do I *what?*"

Mary tilted her head to the side in a look of understanding far beyond her years. "I can tell that you love her. It's fine to say that you do."

Jonathan crossed his arms over his chest. "I don't love her."

But… he just might. He recalled her words that she was falling for *him*. He hadn't wanted to admit it, not even to himself, but he was beginning to feel the same way about her. But he couldn't. Not when he didn't know who she truly was.

"Children…" he said, wiping a hand across his brow, unsure of just how to make them understand. "Miss Donahue… she's not who I thought she was."

"What do you mean?" Matthew asked.

"She's not actually a governess."

That would have to be enough to mollify them.

Mary furrowed her brow. "You mean she is supposed to have a different job?"

"Something like that. She was just pretending."

"But why?"

But why couldn't they just accept what he said as fact? Everyone else in his life did.

"She lied because she wanted the job."

Mary and Matthew looked at one another as they seemed to ponder what he said. Mary spoke first, apparently on behalf of the two of them.

"But she is still our governess, and she is a good governess. So why can't she stay anyway? It doesn't matter that she wasn't a governess before. She is now."

Jonathan opened his mouth and took a breath to respond — until he realized that Mary, actually, had something of a point.

"It's just that she is not who she said she was," he repeated, trying not to let his frustration show. "Who I thought she was."

"But she is still the same person," Mary insisted. "She wasn't acting — was she?"

No. No, she wasn't.

She was still Calli. The Calli that he had gotten to know. The Calli who had broken through all of his barriers. The Calli that he wanted in his life.

Perhaps... perhaps he had been a bit harsh with her.

"You're right," he said, looking at Mary wide-eyed, and the child beamed at him. It was likely the first time he had ever said such a thing to her.

"We best go back and get her," Matthew said, to which Jonathan slowly nodded as hope filled him anew. He still didn't completely trust her... but did he have to say goodbye forever? Maybe she deserved one last chance.

He rapped on the roof of the carriage before sticking his head out the window.

"Johnson — turn around! We've forgotten something."

* * *

Calli's brothers came much sooner than she had been expecting.

"Miss Donahue?" Calli started when the housekeeper found her in Jonathan's study — fortunately, finished putting her plan into action, although she could feel the perspiration sliding down her back from her exertions. It was not exactly a job for one woman, but she had mustered every ounce of strength she possessed in order to carry it out.

It had been worth it.

She had sat down on the chair in front of Jonathan's desk, taking a minute to examine her work.

THE ART OF STEALING A DUKE'S HEART

Mrs. Blonsky seemed slightly perturbed to find her in the study, which was reasonable.

"I was leaving a note for His Grace," Calli explained, motioning to the desk in front of her where there was, fortunately, a neat pile of paper in the middle of the desk. "I might... I might not be here when he returns."

"I see," Mrs. Blonsky said, her smile as present as always, although if Calli wasn't mistaken, she could sense that Mrs. Blonsky might know a bit more than she was letting on. "Very well. You have visitors. I have placed them in the back parlor."

"Thank you, Mrs. Blonsky," Calli said, her heart fluttering as she eyed the rolled piece of canvas in the corner. She could only hope that this would work. Arie and Xander were not easy to fool.

And they would be here now.

Mrs. Blonsky left her to find her own way, which Calli was glad for. She stepped into the parlor to find her two brothers leaning against pieces of furniture.

"You're early," she said by way of greeting, and Arie grinned while Xander still looked somewhat worried.

"Does it matter?" Arie said airily. "We were watching the house. Your duke is gone."

"Yes, he is," Calli said, holding herself up high.

"Where is your bag?"

"Packed, in my room."

"Best go get it. We'll want to leave quickly," Arie said. "And your painting?"

"In the study. Next to the original," she said, her heart beating rapidly at the thought.

"Why don't you lead the way?" Arie said. "Then you can go fetch your things."

"There are a fair number of staff still in the house," Calli said, rubbing her forehead, trying to think of any other way to delay them. "I don't understand why you didn't wait until night, as we agreed upon."

When it would also be darker and harder to see.

"Xander has been watching the house and said that with the duke gone, most of the servants have gone out or are in their living quarters," Arie said. "I figured, why not get a head start?"

"Arie, please, just try to understand where I am coming from in no longer wanting this to happen," she said, desperate to try again. "Can we just leave it?"

He stared at her, unblinking, and Calli wondered for a moment whether her statue of a brother even had a heart.

"I told you the terms, Calli. So — do you want to do this efficiently in a way that he will never know, or would you like him to know all of your betrayal? Your choice."

"Fine," Calli said, trying to release her fists as her stomach turned. "But this must be quick. I shall let you into the study, and then shut the door behind you. As long as no one sees you go in, no one should be the wiser. Just pray a maid doesn't come in to dust while you're there."

Xander gave her a jaunty salute which even Arie rolled his eyes at, before Calli led them slowly down the hall, as though they were breaking into the house and not invited to be here.

Although she didn't think Jonathan would ever invite her brothers into his home, which meant that they were trespassing as much as anyone could ever expect.

She let them into the study, pointed out the painting, and was just about to leave when Xander placed a hand on her arm.

"Calli," he said in a low voice, likely so Arie, across the room, wouldn't hear, "are you all right?"

"Fine," she said, forcing a smile that she knew would be

strained and that Xander would see right through. But now wasn't the time to discuss her feelings. "I'll be back."

She slipped out of the room and down the hall, up the stairs and into her small room. She took one final look around the bedroom and the nursery, her heart breaking with the sadness of never seeing the children nor the house again. She couldn't even think of Jonathan.

She crossed to the schoolroom area of the nursery, taking a slip of paper and a piece of charcoal before dashing off a quick note to Matthew and Mary. Then she crossed the room, quickly unpacked her paint supplies from her bag, and left them out for them. She hoped they would be able to remember her with some fondness.

Calli picked up her bag and hurried down the stairs. She was just about to open the study door when a commotion arose from the front of the house.

"Miss Donahue? Miss Donahue, where are you?"

"Matthew? Mary?" She dropped her bag, her heart hammering in her chest as her joy in seeing them, even for this one last time, fought with her distress as to why they could be here and how she could get her brothers out of the house without anyone else the wiser.

She had to get everyone away from the study.

Calli hurried down the hall to the front foyer, coming to a stop when the children ran toward her, their arms outstretched.

"Miss Donahue! We came back for you!"

She didn't say anything in response — she couldn't, not when her throat was clogged with unshed tears. Finally she looked up from the children, who had their arms wrapped around her, to Jonathan, who stood there, unmoving, his cloak swirled around him imposingly as he stared down at them.

"Your Grace?" she said softly.

He cleared his throat.

"The children are correct. We have returned for you. Perhaps I was too... premature in my conclusions."

"Oh, Jon—Your Grace, I... I don't know what to say."

Her stomach knotted as she thought about what was happening behind her in the house.

Was there a way that she could, potentially, get her brothers out and still go with Jonathan? Could she find a way forward with the man she loved?

For she did. She loved him, despite his obstinance and his distrust and, at times, hardness of heart. She couldn't help herself.

"Just say yes to coming with us, and we can figure out the rest from there."

She stood, nodding, beginning to back out of the foyer.

"I will. Thank you. I just must... go and fetch my things."

She managed a smile before scurrying down the hall, the moment she was around the corner breaking into a run.

Fortunately, there weren't any servants about, and when Calli skidded to a halt in front of the study door, it was just opening.

She wrenched it open, pushing back Xander and Arie, who swore as they stepped back.

She noted the canvas in their hands, looking back and forth from the painting on the wall to the two of them.

"Is it done?" she hissed, and they nodded, although Xander was looking at her somewhat strangely. She ignored him, focused on Arie, for he was always the one to worry about.

"We have a problem," she said, keeping her voice low. "Jonathan is home."

She didn't even care that she had said his given name. Let them think what they wanted. She just needed them gone.

"They've asked me to go with them to Kent, and I'm going

to go," she said resolutely. "I told them I was going to get my bag. Hide in here until you don't hear anything anymore. I'll try to ensure we leave within fifteen minutes. Then you'll have to sneak out on your own — but I'm sure you're both more than adept at doing so."

Xander smirked while Arie looked at her thoughtfully.

"You should come home with us."

"I've made up my mind, Arie," she said, her voice low. "I will come visit upon our return. We shan't be long."

She knew she was likely making the wrong decision. To extend her time with Jonathan was only going to prolong her heartbreak, for there was no way there would ever be room for her in his life as anything more than what she currently was.

But she would take what she could.

She took a deep breath, smoothed her skirts, and opened the door.

Only to come face to face with Jonathan.

CHAPTER 23

When the study door opened to reveal Calli standing there, at first Jonathan's heart leapt, as it always did when he saw her.

But his gut told him something was wrong before his mind caught up.

First, there was her bag sitting outside his study door.

Then, there were her brothers standing behind her.

And in their hands, a rolled-up canvas.

Finally, what should have told him everything, Calli's face — stricken, panicked.

"Calli," he said, hearing the ice dripping off her name as, after his perusal of the room, his gaze returned to her. "Have I interrupted something?"

"It's not what you think," she said, holding up her hands. "Xander and Arie were... helping me when I thought that you no longer wanted my... services."

"Helping you," he repeated incredulously. "Because your little bag and one painting were far too heavy for you?"

She looked at her brothers and then back at him, but before she could say anything, her brother answered for her.

"We were just going, Hargreave," Arie said. "We wanted to check on Calli, that's all. Heard you had been a bit hard on her."

"Hard on her? For lying to me?" Jonathan asked, the thick metal chain tightening within him like a vise. "I don't even know your true name. It certainly isn't Donahue, and Calli tells me it isn't the same as hers."

As her brother's eyes darkened and narrowed, Jonathan looked to Calli, whose eyes widened — in a bit of fear, he realized.

"I'm not sure what my sister told you," Arie bit out, "but I can assure you that there is always one thing that is of my first interest, and that is looking after my siblings. And right now, I don't feel comfortable with my sister going anywhere with you."

"Arie," Calli said, turning around and standing up tall before her brother, "this is my decision."

"And mine," Jonathan cut in. "And before we go any further, I'd like to know just what exactly you are planning to do with that canvas."

He looked to the wall where his painting hung, wondering if he was seeing things, or if it was hanging slightly ajar.

"I told you, Jonathan, it's not what you think," Calli repeated, and he looked to her.

"Just what do you suppose I am thinking? That, perhaps, you recreated a painting in order to switch it with mine, to steal a priceless work? Is that, maybe, what I am thinking?"

"Jonathan," she said desperately, "can I speak to you alone? My brothers were just leaving."

"Not with that painting, they are not," he said, pointing to the floor, ignoring Calli — and all of the feelings within him regarding her — for the moment. "Put it down. Now."

"It's nothing," Arie said easily, "just Calli's little re-creation. You told me yourself that you saw it."

"I don't give a damn what you say," Jonathan seethed. "Leave the painting and get. Out. Now."

"Not without our sister."

"Jonathan—" Calli said, placing a hand on his arm, but he shook her off.

"Not a problem. Take her. She is no longer welcome in my home."

"Jonathan, you don't understand, please let me explain—"

He turned on her now, his voice rising as he spoke until it was nearly a roar.

"I have heard more than enough of your explanations. It is what I see in front of me that tells me more than anything else ever could. You will get out of my house *this instant* before I call the constable on the lot of you. Do you understand?"

"Please," she whispered, her voice so at odds with his.

But Jonathan'd had enough. He couldn't look at her anymore.

"Get out," he said, opening the door. "Go through the servants' entrance so that the children don't see you. Thurston will see you out." He nodded to his waiting butler, who always seemed to know exactly when he was needed. "And never come back."

* * *

CALLI REFUSED to look at either of her brothers on the ride home.

Home. The place where she had spent most of her life. A place that should be comfortable. So why was she dreading returning to it?

She could feel the ice seeping off Arie from across the carriage. She was well aware that he was displeased, although at least he was holding off his lecture until they arrived.

When he would likely deliver it in front of the entire family.

"Calli?"

She lifted her head as Xander placed a hand on her knee.

"Are you all right?" he asked her again, softly.

"No," she said, and while no tears had fallen, kept inside so that Arie wouldn't ridicule her any more than he already had, within her, she was weeping a waterfall. "I am not all right. And nor will I be."

Arie snorted but said nothing as he stared out the window with arms crossed, while Xander looked at her with concern, scratching his head.

"Maybe Diana will know what to do."

"None of you can help me," Calli said bitterly. "You've done more than enough."

They sat in silence for the remainder of the ride, as London turned from the tall imposing brick townhouses of Mayfair to the narrow streets of falling down buildings in St. Giles. Eventually they pulled up in front of the house.

"We will convene in an hour," Arie said, his words clipped as he stepped down from the carriage. "Have yourself ready by then."

Xander held out a hand to help her down, and Calli slowly followed the two of them into the house, her bag swinging against her skirts as she dragged her feet going up the walk.

She didn't feel like facing her family. She didn't feel like discussing everything that had happened. And she most certainly was going to refuse to say anything about Jonathan.

He was unyielding, she realized that. She had known

early on that he was not a man who would easily forgive, if he ever would at all.

She just hadn't realized how irate he would be, to the point that he wouldn't even let her explain. He would never consider anything further with her, she knew that — but at least he would know the truth of what she had done and that, in the end, she could never truly betray him.

As she had her family.

She could never let them know.

Despite her reluctance, an hour later she was seated among her four siblings, as they all sat staring at her with expressions that varied from pity to contempt.

She took the space in the corner of the sofa, hoping that it would swallow her up and she could remain hidden from the rest of them.

Arie stood at the front of the room, arms crossed over his chest as he stared at each of them in turn until his gaze settled on Calli, where it remained.

"As you all know," he began, slowly pacing a few steps back and forth each way as he spoke, "Calli recently undertook her own little… escapade."

He made it sound as though everything that had happened to her was a child's game.

"The initial plan was simple. She was to attend a party held at the duke's townhouse, create a sketch of a painting, noting any necessary details, and then return home to complete the painting. Xander and I were then going to break in and switch the two. No one would ever be the wiser, and we would be able to sell it to a buyer that was already arranged."

Calli couldn't look at him anymore, as she tucked her knees up underneath her chin, hugging her legs against herself.

"However, Calli allowed herself to be caught in the study. By *children*," he said so contemptuously that Calli couldn't help but lift her gaze and glare at him. She had always loved Arie. He was a harsh man, as inflexible as Jonathan, but he loved them in his own way. At the moment, however, she hated him.

"She was mistaken for the governess, a role she accepted, and told us all that she intended to take the time to ensure that her painting was perfect. Well, she was right. It was."

His lips began to stretch into a slow, menacing smile, one that didn't quite reach his eyes. "But then, our Calli did the unthinkable. She fell in love."

Calli pushed herself to her feet then, her hands coming to her hips indignantly, "I did not."

"You didn't?" He lifted a brow. "Or you just didn't think I was aware?"

"How I feel or what I did are of no consequence. None at all. I did what you asked."

"You did, but you fought me every step of the way," Arie said, leaning back against the fireplace behind him as though her words and her ire did not affect him in the least. "You thought you had gotten away with it, but you didn't, did you? Not only did you apparently share some of your true self with this *duke*, but for whatever reason, he seemed to think enough of you to return to London for you, inhibiting all of our plans and ensuring that not only do we not have the painting that we all worked so hard for, but he also has an idea of who we are. He may hate you now, but it never should have gotten to this point."

"You're right," Calli said, angrier now than she had been when it had been Jonathan who was hurling insults upon her. For at least Jonathan had good reason to be upset with her. "I should have stopped this long ago. We had no reason to steal

Jonathan's painting. He did nothing to us, or to your people, Arie."

"Although you did apparently locate one of the priceless artifacts that belonged to my people, and where is that, hmm?"

Calli narrowed her eyes at him.

"You want it so much? Do you? Very well."

She stomped across the room, picking up her bag, taking the stolen figurine and tossing it to him. He gasped before catching it.

"Take it," she said, waving in front of her, "but do not sell it. Give it back to whomever it belongs to. I will not make money off a stolen item."

"It was originally stolen from Greece anyway."

"I understand, Arie," she said, trying to keep the annoyance out of her voice, "but it is not my place to decide whether my wrong is any worse than the original thievery. I'm done with this. All of this. I was only trying to make you happy, to pay you back. You never made me feel adequate enough to belong here."

Even Arie looked slightly stunned at her outburst, as silence settled over the rest of the room. Calli swallowed hard. She hadn't meant to say such things, but it had all come pouring out before she could stop herself.

"Perhaps this wasn't the best time to speak of this," Arie murmured. "We can all meet again tomorrow."

"No!" Calli exclaimed, shaking her head. "I will not meet with you again tomorrow nor the next day nor the day after that. I am done talking about this. I failed. You failed. This was all a mistake."

A lump began to form in her throat as the tears threatened to fall, and she did everything in her power to hold them back.

"I'm sorry I don't fit in this family. But now that we all know the truth, we can move on."

With that, she whirled around and rushed up the stairs to her bedroom, where she slammed the door, knowing she was acting like a child but not at all caring. She finally gave herself over to the pain and let it all flow out in waves.

CHAPTER 24

Jonathan spent a miserable weekend with his mother.

It was always rather miserable to spend more than a day or so in her company. She continually pestered him about when he was going to get married, why he had allowed his sister to leave, and how he was going to properly raise the children.

Of course, this time there were also many questions about why they had arrived without a governess, and just how were they expected to keep the children under control.

So it was with a great deal of relief to return to London while she chose to remain in Kent. He had sent the children to bed early the evening before with Mrs. Blonsky, who suggested that it might be time to hire a new governess, but he had allowed them to eat breakfast with him the following morning.

"Uncle?"

"Yes, Mary?" he said with as much patience as he could muster while he sipped his tea.

"Is Miss Donahue going to come today?"

"No, Mary," he said, shaking his head, steeling his resolve. "Miss Donahue is not here. She lied to us about herself, remember? She has left and she is not coming back."

"Because you told her not to," Matthew said, his arms crossed over his chest. "I heard you."

Jonathan sighed and ran a hand through his hair, realizing that the children were upset and missed their former governess. As did he, if he must admit it to himself. Which he refused to.

"Children," he said, looking them right in the eye, as Calli had always done, "I know you liked Miss Donahue but—"

"We *love* her," Mary cut in.

He cleared his throat. "I know you loved Miss Donahue. But we will find a new governess. One who will be much better for you. One who has proper governess training. One I'm sure you will like just as much."

Mary stared morosely at the untouched plate in front of her.

"No one can ever replace Miss Donahue."

She was right. No one ever would.

"Could we go to the museum today, Uncle?" Matthew asked, breaking the silence, and Jonathan thought on his day ahead. Did he have time to fit in a visit to the museum?

"I have a brief meeting with Mr. Shepherd," he said. "After that, yes, I suppose we can go."

"Hooray!" they cheered, and he had to appreciate how such a simple thing could cause such great excitement.

His man-of-business greeted him with his usual lack of enthusiasm.

"What news have you for me today?"

"The first item is of some interest," Shepherd droned. "You had asked for the canvas to be replaced in its frame." He pointed to the painting above his desk.

"Yes. Was it done?"

"Well," Shepherd scratched at his head, "the thing is, when they went to replace it, they discovered that the original was still in the frame. The other painting was the replicate."

Jonathan stared at him for a moment, trying to make sense of what he was saying.

"So you are telling me that they were leaving with the replicate and not the original?"

"Correct." Shepherd nodded. "The strange thing is, however, the painting had most certainly been tampered with. The canvas is still in good condition, but they had to fix some of the frame."

Jonathan sat back in his chair, rubbing a hand over his eyes.

"That doesn't make any sense."

"No," Shepherd agreed. "The only conclusion they could make was that the painting had already been switched out twice."

"So the replicate had been inserted but then the original already returned?"

Shepherd nodded as Jonathan stared at him in confusion.

"But why would they do such a thing?"

"That, I do not know, Your Grace," he said, shrugging his shoulders. "But rest assured, all is well and there is nothing for you to be concerned about. Would you like to go ahead and press charges?"

Jonathan held up a hand. He might have banished Calli from his life forever, but he would not see her go before the magistrate.

"No," he said, shaking his head. "But if any of them ever return here, you must send word."

"Of course, Your Grace," Shepherd said, checking off the item on the list in front of him before moving on. "Of course."

* * *

Calli stared morosely at the marbles, statues, and other pieces of the Parthenon around her.

She had tried to stay home, citing the fact that she was obviously not fit for such work, anyway. But Arie had told her that she could at least be valuable eyes and ears in his first perusal of the building.

He had a plan — one that had been on his mind for years now — and he was considering whether it was the right time to put it into place.

Calli thought it was foolish. It was one thing to steal from rich noblemen, most of whom would never know the difference. It was quite another to steal from the British government.

But then, Arie insisted that he was only stealing back what belonged to his country, and Calli could see his point. She just didn't have much desire to be involved in his scheme.

Or in much of anything, truth be told. She was still far too distressed upon losing Jonathan. And the children. How their mother ever could have given them up, Calli had no idea. She had spent but a couple of weeks with them and she already missed them fiercely.

"Miss Donahue?"

Calli rubbed her temples. She was so far into her morose musings that she was hearing things. Hearing the children's voices. Or perhaps they were simply memories that wouldn't leave her be. She couldn't be certain.

"Miss Donahue, is that you?"

"Shh, Mary, get back here!"

Calli whirled around to find the two blond children racing down the marbled hall toward her, ignoring the call of the maid behind them who was trying to keep up as a museum employee frowned at them.

Calli looked around both warily and hopefully for Jonathan but, not seeing him, crouched down and wrapped one arm around each child.

"Oh, Mary, Matthew, it is so good to see you," she said, closing her eyes as she relished the moment before leaning back to look at the two of them. "How are you?"

"We miss you," Matthew said, sticking out his bottom lip, and Calli's heart broke a little bit at the emotion from the boy who always tried so hard to keep it within, to prove how grown up he was.

"I know," Calli said, resting back on her heels as she looked at them. "I miss you too."

"Can you come back?" Mary asked. "Please?"

Calli sighed inwardly as she attempted to keep the smile on her face.

"I'm not sure what your uncle told you," she said slowly, "but I am no longer able to work as your governess. I thought I could take on that role for you, but I... well, I made a mess of things."

"Uncle said that you aren't who you said you were," Matthew said, crossing his arms over his chest, "but I told him that you are still the person you always seemed to be, on the inside, where it mattered."

Calli attempted to hold back the tears that threatened to spill over.

"I know, but I hurt your uncle. I broke his trust. That is quite difficult to recover."

"I don't know why he says that," Mary burst in, "because he is sad too. He has been sad since you left. He's even worse than he was before you came. And, we had to go spend time with our grandmother."

She rolled her eyes so dramatically that it was difficult for Calli not to laugh.

"Well, I'm sure your grandmother appreciated the visit," Calli said. "As for your uncle…"

"He loves you, Miss Donahue," Mary insisted. "I know he does."

Calli looked down as the emotion threatened to overcome her. Could he actually love her, feel anything but hatred for her, after all they had been through, all that she had done? Could she forgive him for not having any faith in her at all?

Of course she would. For she loved him.

And while she knew they would never have a future together, she had to find a way to at least make him see that she would never betray him, that she wasn't the woman he assumed her to be.

How she was going to do it, she had no idea. But she had to try.

"Mary, Matthew," their maid stood behind them, a pleading expression on her face as she looked around, "we really must get back to your uncle. He will be waiting as we were only supposed to be gone for a few minutes."

Jonathan was here? Calli's heart quickened. She wouldn't see him now, not with the children present, but the thought of him so close was enough to make her tremble anew.

"It was ever so lovely to see you," Calli told them, placing a hand on each of their shoulders. "I don't know when we will have the chance again, but hopefully sometime soon."

"Goodbye, Miss Donahue," they said in unison, and Calli didn't have the heart to correct them as they turned and walked away.

* * *

Jonathan watched the children's amazement as they gazed upon the various wonders of the world.

Wonders all contained here in the museum.

Mary, Matthew, and the maid had all acted somewhat strangely when they returned from their foray to the Greek exhibit, but now they seemed quite caught up with the sarcophaguses and sculptures of the Egyptian room.

Jonathan watched them with his arms behind his back. He had to admit that this wasn't such a bad idea. He couldn't remember the last time he had been to the museum, nor paid any attention to the exhibits. Seeing it through the children's eyes brought everything to life in a way he hadn't entirely considered possible.

"Well, if it isn't the duke."

Jonathan turned at the deep voice behind his ear, finding Calli's eyes looking back at him — only they were out of very masculine face.

"Xander." He turned his gaze back around to watch the children. "Did you follow me here?"

Calli's brother snorted. "What reason would I have to follow *you* around? I have much better things to do with my time."

"Perhaps for the same reason you had your sister pretend to be a governess in my home?"

Xander inclined his head. "I can see why you might think that. There is something you should know, however. Calli never really wanted to be part of this. It's a family business, as you may have determined by now. This painting was her first real chance to prove herself. But once she started working for you, getting to know you and the children... well, she tried countless times to cry off."

"Yet she still went through with it."

Jonathan refused to be moved by this man's words. He

had no idea why Xander was here, defending his sister, but he didn't have to stay here and listen to it.

"If you'll excuse me, I must—"

"She only went through with it because Arie threatened to reveal all if she didn't. And she didn't think you would ever forgive her." His lips twisted into a wry grimace. "I'm assuming she was right about that."

Jonathan took a breath, attempting to rein in his ire. Of course this man was right. Who would have patience for a woman who pretended to be someone she was not, who attempted to steal a painting worth thousands of pounds?

"She told you what she could, when she could. And in the end? She outsmarted Arie, in order to protect you."

Jonathan whipped around, his gaze boring into the other man, even as he knew already, deep within him, what he was about to say.

"What are you talking about?"

Xander looked from side to side as though someone might overhear before stepping up to Arie. "I know Calli's work. It may look identical to the original painting to everyone else, but she's been painting since she was old enough to hold a brush in her hand, and I know that the painting that was already hanging on the wall was hers. I don't know how she did it, but she switched out the paintings before we even got there, so the painting that would remain was your original."

Jonathan searched Xander's face, trying to determine if there was any artifice there, but he was either a talented actor… or he was telling the truth.

A truth that Jonathan already knew. He had known it as soon as Shepherd told him that the painting was the true one, that it had already been switched out at least twice.

"I don't understand… at some point she would have been found out."

Xander shrugged. "It would have been too late by then. Arie would have been irate — he already was with the result as it is — but he would never hurt her, nor turn her out. He loves her too much."

A frown pinched Jonathan's forehead.

Xander must have noted the expression on Jonathan's face. "As a sister."

Jonathan stood, silently contemplating all that this man — this thief — had told him. It didn't make a difference, did it? Could it? But he supposed he was glad to know it.

"Well," Xander said, apparently seeing that Jonathan wasn't going to say anything else. "Now you know. And the other thing? My sister is miserable without you. I've told her that you don't deserve her, but?" He threw his hands in the air. "Who am I to instruct the heart?"

And at that he began to walk away, whistling as he went.

Jonathan could only stare after him.

CHAPTER 25

Calli had put brush to paper, unsure what was going to come out the end.

Now she stared at the scene in front of her, closing her eyes to hold back the tears.

For it was the land. The land in Kent. The land that she had ridden with Jonathan and the children. Oh, what a day that had been. It was, she realized now with surprise, one of the happiest days of her life. Which was ridiculous. She had a family who loved her, who would do anything for her, and here she was, longing for a man who hated her.

There was no reason for it, and she was disgusted with herself. She was weak.

She did, however, have an idea on just how she would tell Jonathan the truth.

She found another piece of paper, only this time she dipped her pen in ink and set it to the paper.

On it, she told him all that had happened, all that she had done, all that she was sorry for. She could only hope he would read it, so that, at the very least, he would understand that she had never betrayed him.

Once the paint dried, she bound it all up in a large package, then sent it with a boy, along with a few coins. She placed her hands on her hips and let out an audible sigh as she watched him skip down the street with it. She had promised him further payment when he returned and told her who he had given it to. At least then she would know that it had arrived.

She only wished she could know Jonathan's reaction when it did.

* * *

HE STARED down at the painting before him. It was Kent. It was his land. The land that he had always loved, but now, after being there with the children, he realized how much it meant to him, how good it had felt to get out of London and spend time there, where he could let go of everything that bound and held him here in the city.

There he was free.

The work was masterful, and would be worthy of a place on any of his walls, in his gallery or, better yet, somewhere that all could enjoy.

Except that he couldn't have it anywhere that would taunt him, reminding him of all he'd had, and all he had lost.

He had known it was her work that moment he had opened the package. A package delivered by a boy, he was told, which was addressed to him and him only.

It was then that he noticed the scrap of paper that had fallen out, and he picked it up to find steady, strong handwriting upon the note.

A note that told him everything her brother had divulged.

She finished by saying that she expected nothing more from him. Only that she needed him to know the truth. That she loved him and would never do anything to hurt him.

Jonathan lowered his head into his hands, looking down at the desk below him. The desk which now held her painting, a painting which would always be priceless in his mind. For no one could ever so properly replicate the peace that he felt within his heart in one image.

Suddenly his gaze was caught by something in the detail of the painting. He squinted his eyes to better see. Was he only imaging it?

No, there it was. On the horizon of the image, there were four shapes — silhouettes, really, of four people, holding hands as they looked out on all before them. Two adults and two children. The four of them.

Jonathan let out a groan as he threw himself back in his chair and closed his eyes to the painting, not wanting to see it anymore. Only then he not only saw the image, but more. He saw the four of them, in color, joy on their faces as they ran over the fields. Mary. Matthew. Him. Calli.

He tried to replace her face with another's. After all that he had come to know about her, he should find another woman. But would he ever find anyone else he could be happy with?

No. He absolutely could not. Calli was it for him. She had ruined him for all others.

And, he realized slowly as he came to stand, running a hand through his hair, that was just fine.

For he loved her. He loved her as she apparently did him.

Yes, she was from a family of thieves. Yes, she had deceived him. But in the end, he could no longer deny that she had done what she'd thought was right.

Jonathan hurried around the desk, suddenly knowing what he needed to do. He needed to make things right. And he needed to win back the woman he loved.

He started calling for Thurston, Mrs. Blonsky, and Shepherd. He needed all of their help if he was going to do this the right way.

And he needed the help of two very important people. Two people, he was sure, who would be quite pleased with his decision.

* * *

"CALLIOPE MURPHY."

"Yes, Diana?"

Calli looked up from her painting to find her sister framed in the doorway.

"Is something wrong?" she asked.

"Yes, something is most certainly wrong," Diana said, crossing the room to take a seat in the chair beside Calli, her skirts flouncing up in a huff that she apparently felt herself. "I am done with this."

"With what?"

"With your moping around, hiding in your room, pining after a duke who was never yours to begin with. It's time to lift your bodice back up and return to being the Calli that we all know and love."

Calli straightened, setting her paintbrush down before turning to Diana.

"Diana, you have no idea what you are talking about."

"I believe I do. You haven't been the same since you returned."

"No," Calli said, shaking her head, a small, sad smile crossing her face. "You are right. I have not. And you know what the truth is? I will likely never be the same again."

Diana opened her mouth, but Calli held up a hand, stopping her flow of words.

"That doesn't mean that I am not happy or will never know joy. It's just... I've learned so much. I've learned about love. I've learned about myself. I know what makes me happy now."

"Your duke?" Diana said wryly, and Calli inclined her head as she studied her sister, the only fair-haired one of them all.

"He did make me happy, yes. As did the children. But I am no fool. I have not allowed all of my hopes to rest on him. No, what makes me happy is painting — but painting my own work."

"You already knew that."

"Yes, but now I'm wondering — can I make a life for myself as a painter? Should I try to sell some of these? I know they litter the walls of the house, as well as the floors underneath the beds, but maybe… maybe people might actually like them. The duke was as fine of an art connoisseur as anyone I have ever met. He saw some of my work and he actually had high praise."

Diana lifted a brow. "I do not mean to discredit you here, Calli, as I am well aware of your talent. But did he say he liked your paintings because he wanted to sleep with you, or because he wanted to hang them on his walls?"

Calli's cheeks immediately heated, but she refused to allow Diana to get under her skin.

"He is not the type of man who would say such a thing just as a compliment. He says what he means."

"Well," Diana said with a shrug. "It's worth a try, I suppose. But how would you even do such a thing, especially as a woman, and one without any connections at that?"

"I'm not sure about that yet," Calli said with a sigh. "Maybe Arie can help me."

"Maybe," Diana said, although she didn't sound entirely confident.

"Calli?" Damien stood at the door, a slip of paper in his hand. "A note came for you."

"For me?" she said with a frown, unsure of who would ever have need of her beyond those that lived in this house. She rose and took the paper from him, her eyes skimming over the words in familiar handwriting. Handwriting that she had taught herself.

Come quickly, Miss Donahue, we have urgent need of you. Mary and Matthew

"I must go," she said, flying to the peg on the wall for her cloak.

"Go where?" Diana asked, but Calli was already out the door, leaving her siblings behind. She had no need nor time to explain to them. They wouldn't understand, anyway.

"Calli?" Xander appeared now, and her steps slowed. She would never be able to completely ignore Xander, no matter the circumstance. Their bond was too strong.

She held out the note to him, pleading at him with her eyes, silently begging for him to understand.

He did. He looked up at her and nodded. "I'll go with you."

"Go where?" Diana cried after them, but Xander simply called behind him, "We'll return shortly," and Calli gratefully followed him out the doors toward the stable at the back.

When they arrived at Jonathan's townhouse, the carriage had barely come to a stop before Calli was out onto the street and flying up the steps. When she knocked and no one answered, the fears that she had been trying to tamp down all the way here began to rise within her, but Xander placed a hand on her shoulder and she calmed — slightly.

Finally, Thurston opened the door, surprisingly not shocked to find Calli and her brother standing there.

"Miss Donahue," he said with a slight bow, "please, come in."

"Mary? Matthew?" she asked him, her heart still pounding. "Are they all right?"

"Indeed," he said. "Please follow me."

Calli shared a bewildered glance with Xander before the two of them followed the butler, who was walking far too slowly for her liking, down the hall toward the back parlor — the one which overlooked the small garden at the back that Calli had always enjoyed.

The butler stopped in front of the door, but instead of entering to announce her, he swept his hand out toward the door, bidding her to enter.

Calli did so trepidatiously — only for her mouth to drop open at what she saw within.

Next to the window was an easel, the canvas already laid out upon it, awaiting color, causing her fingers to twitch.

A desk sat next to it, filled with every color of paint one could ever imagine, from the color of the sky to the murky ocean. Brushes of every size, every shape were lined up neatly, with a comfortable-looking leather tufted chair in the middle, facing out between the canvas and the window beyond.

Beside this most beautiful display were two smaller replications of it.

And in the corner of the room, an even more incredible sight — Jonathan, standing behind Mary and Matthew, one hand on each of their shoulders.

"Calli?" Mary said, a wide smile on her face, "may I call you that?"

"Of course," Calli said after clearing her throat, finding that she had lost her voice for a moment as she was so overcome by all in front of her.

"What do you think?"

"I think… this looks amazing," she said, forcing a smile onto her face. "You are the luckiest children I know."

"Yes," Mary persisted, "we are looking forward to painting here, 'tis true. But what do *you* think?"

"I think I can hardly wait to see what you come up with," Calli said, wondering just why they had called her here, what they expected of her. Jonathan had obviously known about this scheme for her to arrive at the house, but why was he just standing there, doing nothing, saying nothing?

"Mary, Matthew," Jonathan said, crouching down, "I'm not sure that Calli quite understands. Why don't you go play for a moment while I talk to her?"

The children looked somewhat crestfallen, but nodded and left the room, as Xander stared at the two of them unsurely.

"I'll ah, go keep an eye on them," he said.

Calli nodded to him gratefully, glad that he was here, that she knew she always had him to lean on.

"Calli," Jonathan began, stepping toward her, but Calli held up a hand.

"Let me go first — please?" she said imploringly, and he paused but then nodded.

"I know you've received my letter and already know all that I ever wanted you to," she said. "But there was one thing I never did say properly. And that is that I am sorry. I never meant for this — any of this — to happen."

"I know," he said with a small smile. "You are a good person, Calli, I know that. I realize that. And I never gave you a chance."

"But—"

He was the one to hold up a hand now, just as she noted her painting — the one she had sent him — hanging behind him on the wall.

"You learned rather quickly, I'm afraid, that I am a man who often allows his temper to get the best of him. That I like to get my way and am not pleased at anyone who stands up to me. That I do not trust easily and refuse to allow the trust to return once it has been broken."

Calli listened, inwardly agreeing with him. He was right. He was all of those things. And yet she loved him anyway.

"When you weren't who you said you were I felt… betrayed." He turned from her for a moment, running a hand through his hair, and Calli's heart ached at the pain on his face. Pain that she had caused. "I lashed out against you, forced you out of my house, out of my heart."

"I understand why you did what you did, Jonathan," she murmured. "There is no need to feel badly about it."

"Except that I was wrong."

Her head shot up at that, and now he was taking her hands in his, those crystal blue eyes of his boring into hers with more intense an expression than she had ever seen before.

Her mouth rounded as she tried to say something — anything — but nothing would come out.

"I should have given you a chance. I know what you did, how you tried to keep me from losing the painting. I knew the second Shepherd told me the original was still in the frame, and yet, still, I refused to believe."

"You had every right—"

"No," he squeezed her hands gently. "I should have trusted in what I felt for you. The connection we had. The one that was never a lie, even though your name was."

Calli felt the tears beginning to form, but she pushed a watery smile onto her face.

"I've always been Calli," she managed, her words just over a whisper.

"I know," he said, pulling her closer. "This room — I want it to be yours. I want you to have the freedom to paint, but to paint what you want to paint. To paint original works, that will become renowned throughout the world."

"How did you know?" she choked out.

"Know what?"

"My dream?"

"I didn't," he said, frowning, "I just thought... if this was where your passion lay, why not chase it?"

"So you want me to return as the children's governess?" she asked, unclear just why this room was set up in his townhouse.

"Their governess?" he said, his eyes widening, and then laughed lightly. "Absolutely not."

"But—"

"Calli," he said, lowering himself to one knee before her, "I want you to be my wife."

CHAPTER 26

She didn't say anything.

Why wasn't she saying anything?

She was just staring at him with those luminous violet eyes, covered in a sheen of water. Jonathan wasn't sure whether she was happy or upset or unsure.

"Calli?" he said, squinting up at her. "Are you—"

"Oh, Jonathan," she whispered, tugging him to his feet. "Are you sure?"

"Am I sure?"

"I'm not exactly duchess material," she said, laughing self-consciously. "My family are thieves, if you haven't realized that by now. I come from nothing. I am no one."

"You are Calli — hopefully soon to be Calli Saville, Duchess of Hargreave," he said fiercely, insistently, needing her to understand. "If you will say yes. If you can't — I understand. I'm not the easiest of men, I know that. I work too hard, too often, forget to enjoy life. But you have shown me what is most important. I love you, Calli. No other woman will ever take your place in my heart. It's just not possible."

She stared at him then, clutching the sleeves of his jacket as though she needed to hold onto him to stay upright.

And then she launched herself into his arms and kissed him with all of the ferocity he knew she held deep within her.

Finally she eased back from him, staring up at him with a smile on her face.

"Is that a yes?" he asked, raising his brows, to which she laughed.

"A thousand times yes," she said, before leaning in to kiss him once more.

It didn't last long as a knock sounded on the door, and two voices called within.

"Did she say yes?"

"Are you going to be married?"

"Yes," Jonathan said, finally allowing the smile of happiness and relief to grow on his face. "She said yes."

Another frame filled the doorway — one as tall as Jonathan, and even broader. Calli's brother looked at the scene in front of him, his face uneasy for a moment. Jonathan met his eye and gave him a nod — a nod that told him that yes, he would take care of his sister, that there was no need to worry.

Finally, the man's lips tilted upward into the smallest of smiles — although it was, nevertheless, a smile. Jonathan would take it.

"Xander," Calli said, leaving Jonathan for a moment to extend her hand to her brother, "come in."

"I was just having quite an important lesson on the frogs that now live in the pond outside," Xander said, to which Calli laughed before she looked down at the children, an answering smile on her face to theirs.

She placed a hand on Jonathan's chest, and he knew what she was thinking — by marrying, they were not only committing to one another. They were committing to this family. Jonathan had always been scared to allow his heart to become this full, had always been sure that something would come along and take it all away if he allowed it to do so.

But now… now he knew that love was stronger than that. And he had Calli to thank for it.

"Well," Xander said as he looked at the pair of them, "This will be a wedding unlike anything London has ever seen before."

"Yes," Calli said as she smiled up at Jonathan, and he ran a hand over her curls, "It most certainly will."

* * *

Calli had been right.

St. George's had likely never seen such a wide array of guests as they had when Calliope Murphy wed Jonathan Saville, Duke of Hargreave. How the nobility would have felt to know they were actually sitting but a pew away from some of London's most prolific of thieves, Jonathan wasn't sure.

But he wasn't about to tell any of them.

He and Arie had sat down after the proposal to discuss the arrangement. Calli had felt it quite unnecessary, but Arie had insisted, and Jonathan had agreed it might be prudent.

The arrangement, however, had nothing to do with the marriage.

No, it was about Arie's 'business' and how it would affect his sister in the future.

The terms had been simple. While Jonathan would never prevent Calli from seeing her family, she was to have no part in their thievery. Arie would not share his plans with her, nor would ask for her support in anything. Calli and Jonathan's connections would not be used to help Arie gain any advantage, and nor would they ever come after any of Jonathan's friends or family.

Arie hadn't seemed thrilled with some of it, but he had, eventually, agreed.

After giving Calli away, he had sat with his arms crossed and stared Jonathan down, but Jonathan had barely noticed. Not when he saw Calli. She was every bit the Greek goddess he had always thought her to be, shocking the *ton* by wearing her hair flowing down her back in loose curls. Her long white dress, airy and flowy, made him think of her tossed back among his sheets, and he had to concentrate to remember where he was and the importance of this part of their union.

The rest would come later.

It went by quickly, the only part Jonathan truly remembered was the end — when he whispered "I love you" to his new bride and then escorted her out of the church.

For the first time in his life, everything was finally as it was meant to be.

* * *

"Was that not the most entertaining breakfast?" Calli asked as Jonathan opened the doors to his bedroom, a place Calli remembered with the fondest of memories. She walked over to the bed, trailing her fingers down the coverlet, remembering... and anticipating.

"The part where Matthew placed pudding on your sister's dining chair, or when Xander began to openly flirt with the Marchioness of Crawford?"

Calli turned as Jonathan shut the door, finding that he was already removing his cravat.

"I was thinking more so of when your mother began to question Arie about what he did for a living. She would make the most proficient of investigators. Even Arie was sweating."

"Or when Damien used the serving spoon for his soup."

"Or when my husband made the most beautiful toast. One that nearly had me rising from the table and leading you up here hours ago."

Jonathan's chuckle was not exactly humorous, but rather… seductive.

Calli lost her own smile as she swallowed hard.

"Having children in the house did not exactly make it easy for me to sneak you away, although I tried awfully hard throughout the day."

"I know you did," she said, trailing a finger over his chin, where the slightest bit of stubble was already beginning to make an appearance.

"For a man of such control, you weren't exactly… subtle."

"No man could be. Not with you."

She smiled widely at him as she stepped closer and wrapped her arms around his neck, tilting her head back to look up at him.

"Why, thank you, Your Grace."

"Is there really need for such formalities here, Your Grace?"

"I think not," she said, tsking like any good governess would do. "No formalities here. Most especially that cravat."

She began to tug at it, struggling slightly, but he allowed her to continue until finally she had completely freed it and thrown it on the floor.

"Just the cravat?" he asked teasingly, although his eyes flashed.

"Your boots most certainly have to go."

"Certainly."

He crouched down and swiftly unlaced them, kicking them off before holding out a hand to her. "Your slippers."

"Very well," she said, and caught her bottom lip between her teeth as he slid them off slowly and sensuously.

She continued to instruct him until he was clad in only his breeches, and she swallowed as she stared at him, tracing a line down the indent between his muscles.

"I feel rather underdressed," Jonathan said, stepping toward her.

"Is there anything I can do to help?" she asked, arching an eyebrow.

"Perhaps by dressing a slight bit more informally yourself," he said, sliding his hands along her side before slipping them behind her, finding her buttons and pushing them through the small hooks.

She arched into him, allowing him to do so, until the dress pooled at her feet in a white silk waterfall.

"No stays," she said, lifting her hands. "Rather informal, wouldn't you think?"

Jonathan didn't answer her, his ability to speak apparently having fled as he took her in his arms and kissed her, lavishing her with his tongue, his lips, promising her forever and more.

Calli nearly dissolved at his touch, losing all her thought as he tugged her backward toward the bed behind her, before laying her down upon it.

They broke from one another to divest themselves of the rest of their clothing before she scooted backward on the bed and they continued their loving exploration.

Whereas the last time had been a discovery of one another and shock at the fiery explosion that had erupted between them, now it was a demand for more, along with the knowledge that this was not the last time — it was only the beginning.

Jonathan readied her with his mouth, his fingers, until

Calli was writhing beneath him, desperate for more, for all that he could offer her.

And finally when he entered her, she wrapped her arms around him, knowing she was complete, that she had found herself and her purpose.

As they came together in joyous celebration, she knew that nothing was ever going to be the same again — and she couldn't be happier about it.

EPILOGUE

Calli sat on the edge of the picnic blanket, watching as Matthew and Mary ran around in circles, arms outstretched as they lifted their faces to the sun.

She and Jonathan shared a smile.

"You're happy here?" he asked, his arm coming around her, and she leaned back into him.

"Of course," she said, tilting her head back lazily to look up at him, "I'm happy wherever you are."

"But here, in Kent, away from London," he insisted, "you're not bored?"

"On the contrary," she said. "The children seem much freer here, more themselves. I find inspiration everywhere. And I have much more time with my husband."

Jonathan smiled ruefully, and Calli placed a hand on his knee, knowing that look.

"Don't apologize, Jonathan. I know that you have many responsibilities."

"I do," he acknowledged. "But you, Mary, and Matthew, will always come first. You know that, don't you?"

"I do," she said. "But you need to find room for more."

"What do you mean?" he said, frowning. "Nothing else could come before you."

"Not come before us," she amended, "but *with* us."

She moved his hand and placed it on her stomach. "We shall have another addition to our family very soon."

He stilled in shock, and Calli nearly laughed at the expression on his face.

"Are you sure?"

"Absolutely sure," she said. "How do you feel about it?"

"I—I feel…" He didn't seem to have anything else to say, and Calli did laugh this time.

"You feel, Jonathan, and that is the most important thing."

He nodded slowly and Calli leaned back into him once more.

"Have you told anyone else?" He asked. "Your family? Diana?"

"No," she shook her head, "You first, of course. I will tell Xander when he comes to visit."

That was right. Her brother was coming to stay with them for a week. That should be interesting. At least it wasn't Arie.

"We'll tell Mary and Matthew first," she said.

Jonathan nodded as the children began to chase one another over the field. "I agree."

"I heard a rather interesting rumor from the magistrate's wife down the road."

"Oh, did you now?"

Calli nodded. "Apparently there has been quite the rise in thefts of Greek statues throughout London. From both private residences and public galleries."

"Goodness," Jonathan murmured, "I wonder who that could be."

Calli studied him.

"Did you know anything about it?"

"When your brother and I discussed the marriage," he said, and Calli could tell he was choosing his words carefully, "we decided that it was best he kept his... business to himself."

Calli frowned, for a moment not entirely pleased at being left out of such a decision. But she realized what it must mean, for Jonathan to be tied to such a family, and the position it would place both of them in for her to have knowledge that she couldn't exactly share with him — or anyone else.

"I think that was the right decision."

"You do?" Hope lit Jonathan's eyes, and Calli realized that he had been struggling in keeping this from her.

"I do," she said firmly. "I will always remain close to my family, but I never wanted to be part of that side of their lives anyway. Now I can have the best of them without the rest of it."

Jonathan placed a kiss behind her ear, causing a tingle to run through her.

"There's something else."

"Oh?"

"Do you remember the art dealer I sent some of your paintings to?"

"Yes." Calli's heart quickened.

"He'd like to see more. He said he has buyers."

"He does?" Calli twisted around, trying not to allow too much hope to invade, but unable to keep it away. "Does he know that I — a woman — painted them?"

"He does. You are a duchess so that helps things as well."

"Did you tell him that?"

"I told him you were my wife. He said, however, his buyer has no idea of your identity — that he saw the paintings in his office and told him to 'name the price.' It is your work, Calli. It has nothing to do with your title or your name."

"Thank you, Jonathan," she said, placing her hand in his and squeezing his fingers tight. "For everything."

"It is you I have to thank," he said, placing a kiss on the top of her head, "for showing me what life is about. What love really means. What's important."

She turned her head and gave him her lips.

For he already had her heart. Her trust. Her love.

No matter what.

THE END

* * *

Sign-up for Ellie's email list and "Unmasking a Duke," a regency romance, will come straight to your inbox — free!

www.elliestclair.com/ellies-newsletter

You will also receive links to giveaways, sales, updates, launch information, promos, and the newest recommended reads.

VOLUME ONE

Preview Xander & Juliet's story, book 2 in the Thieves of Desire series…

CHAPTER 1

SUSSEX ~ 1813

Xander danced around the outskirts of the ballroom, only his feet weren't in time with the music.

He caught Damien's eye from across the room. They nodded at one another, acknowledging both the role they were playing as well as their true purpose for being here.

A woman nudged against Xander's side, and he murmured an apology, aware that it was not his place to be knocking over guests. Only when she looked up at him from beneath fluttering lashes, Xander realized that it had not been an accident whatsoever. He flashed her an appreciate smile, but he had no time for flirting.

Not tonight, at least.

He lifted his tray as one of the guests placed his drink upon it, and then continued on through the room, remembering all his eldest brother, Arie, had taught him about the nobility and the role he would play as a footman in one of their houses.

The house was owned by a man who was by no means ultimately one of the highest-ranking men of England, but one of the richest. He had, apparently, done an excellent job over the years of gathering the debts of more than one poor bloke who'd lost far too much at the gambling table. Now the baron owned half of London, most of whom were here tonight despite their lack of goodwill towards him.

"How is the evening?" Damien asked as they passed one another, and Xander merely shrugged. He could think of other ways his night could be better spent, but there were far worse things one could be doing to make a living.

Such as actually working as a footman, spending his life doing another man's bidding for minimal compensation.

No, thank you.

If all worked out here — and he was sure it would for every one of Arie's plans was carefully cultivated, particularly after that one disastrous night five years ago — he and his family would be even richer than they already were.

Xander couldn't stop his eyes from straying to the necklines of women who passed. He wasn't focused on the ample decolletage spilling from the tops of their nearly translucent gowns, however.

Now, he was far more focused on all that sparkled above them — earrings, necklace, and brooches, with the odd ring that flashed as a hand raised a drink to lips.

It was a shame, really, that the style of the day was for minimal jewels, for far too many were tucked away, not available for others to appreciate.

And yet, that was also one of the reasons he had the opportunity to find all of the baron's collection — together, at once — and add to his riches.

Fingers trailed along the back of his neck, and Xander involuntarily shivered as he turned to find an older woman eyeing him with obvious interest. Perhaps the role of a footman wouldn't be so bad after all, he pondered, for there seemed to be plenty of opportunity to avail himself to what these women had to offer — although he wasn't speaking of their affections but rather what they wore. Xander had always had an eye for the finery.

But not tonight.

Tonight he had to maintain his head, to keep his attention on all before him, for there was a much bigger prize available to him. It would require a great deal more time and would not be nearly as fun in achieving, but it would be worth it in the end.

He was told that the Harold Raymond, Baron of Wilington, was going to be married soon, that he was courting a woman years younger than himself, one with little prospects but a beauty like no other. Whether she would truly become his wife or instead his mistress, the baron apparently didn't entirely care. Raymond had no shame, nor any reason to worry about making a misstep. He was too old to care, and besides, he already had the rest of them in his palm.

Xander would have admired him had he not treated his staff like dirt and considered himself a gift to all of humanity.

"John, over here!"

Xander turned, remembering *he* was John. Truth be told, all the footmen in the house were John, as the baron had no care to actually remember any of their names. Which was just fine with him, for it meant that when he was gone with what he came for, no one would remember him or Damien or just what they had been doing in the house.

"Champagne!" the baron called as Xander neared him. The baron stood close to the side of the dance floor, although Xander doubted the man ever wandered onto it himself anymore. Beside him was a man near Xander's age, black hair slicked back over his head as his stare wandered appreciatively over the woman who stood across from the baron, her back to Xander. The back of her neck was long and pale, the slim curve of her shoulders covered just at the top where they delicately arched beneath the cream fabric of her dress. Despite Xander's lack of attraction to his other propositions tonight, he had to fight the urge to reach out and trail his fingers along the woman's soft skin. Xander spotted what he was sure would be two long jewels hanging from her ears, framing her honey brown hair was loosely tied in a chignon above her neck. That color of hair... it was one he would always be drawn to, that he could never forget. Not after *her*.

He shook his head to clear it as he stepped forward, lowering the tray between the baron and the woman. He knew he should keep his gaze demure, lowered, but he couldn't help but lift his head to see what this woman might look like from the front. Would she be anything like the woman who insisted on haunting his dreams at night?

As her fingers curled around the glass and she lifted it to her lips, he looked up, meeting her eyes — and stilled in shock when their gazes collided, as the glass tumbled from her fingers, shattering all over the floor.

~~~~~

JULIET FROZE. She felt the smooth glass slipping out of her hand, heard it shatter across the marble at her feet, allowed the drops of liquid to splash across her dress, likely ruining it.

But she couldn't look away as she gazed into the eyes of the man she'd never thought she would see again.

No, make that the man she *vowed* to never see again. The

man who had taken everything from her. The man who had abandoned her. The man who had broken her heart.

She likely would have remained there, a statue, had Lord Wilington not started bellowing from across from her.

"Juliet! Look what you've done. And you," he rounded his red, sputtering gaze onto Xander, who was the first to recover as he tore his eyes away from her, "what were you thinking?"

"My apologies, my lord," Xander said, dipping his head in a manner very un-like the Xander that Juliet had known. Or the man she had thought she had known. "I should have caught it."

"Yes, you should have. Now, clean this up."

"Of course, my lord."

He turned around and began walking away, as Juliet finally looked down at herself. She needed to clean up, yes, but more importantly, she needed a moment to compose herself, to recover from the shock of seeing *him*. Here.

"Excuse me, my lord, but I should retire for a moment."

She turned before the baron could say anything, practically running from the ballroom despite the many eyes that turned to look at her. Eyes that she was already used to. She knew how uncommon it was for a woman without title or noble blood besides the distant relatives she claimed to be considered as a potential bride of a man like the baron. But her story was that her father was a wealthy merchant, which the baron seemed fine with. He cared much more for money than title. His wife had died years ago and he had no care for propriety. He liked to have a woman — a much younger woman — on his arm, to keep up appearances and to show off his vast collection of jewels, if nothing else. He enjoyed being envied, being feared.

Which was exactly what Juliet was hoping for. She needed more time here. More time to finish her task, to find what she was looking for. The last thing she needed was complications.

Complications like Xander Murphy.

She hurried down the hall, around the corner to the stairway, where one of the maids eyed her with contempt. She understood. She was living the life of a woman of loose morals — even if she hadn't actually taken part in the acts that granted one the title.

Not only that, but she was here — for tonight at least — in the house of a baron, being paraded around as his woman. He didn't care much of what anyone thought, but told her that he preferred to have her close by.

Even if it was only for her to show off his collection of jewels and look after him, like a nanny would a young child.

Just as Juliet rounded the corner and opened up the door to her room, a strong hand grabbed her arm, and she whirled around, ready to fight or to scream, she wasn't sure which.

But instead, she found her heart beating wildly for an altogether different reason as she was trapped within arms that were both familiar and all too welcome when she should have been cursing them.

"Xander," she practically whispered, unable to say his name in fill volume. "What are you doing?"

"What am *I* doing?" he hissed, and it was then she saw the storm in his eyes, those eyes that were such a unique shade of blue they were near to purple and far too beautiful for a man. "I was going to ask you the same thing."

Not thinking about her actions, she took his hand in hers and tugged him into her bedroom, looking furtively up and down the hall before she closed the door behind him.

"Aren't you supposed to be cleaning up my glass?" she asked, cloaking her distress and placing her hands on her hips as she turned to look at him. He was dressed in the baron's livery, although she would most certainly would have remembered had she seen him around the house before.

"Damien's taking care of it," he muttered.

"Damien's here too?" Juliet asked in surprise before she narrowed her eyes at Xander. "What are you two up to?"

"What are we up to?" he asked incredulously. "Don't tell me that you are actually here because you're sleeping with that awful, decrepit old man."

Juliet placed her hands on her hips, shuddering at the thought of it. "If I was — which I'm not — but even if I was, what business is it of yours?"

"I—" Xander opened his mouth to answer her, but shut it firmly, turning around as he ran a hand through his dark hair — which was far too long and was now beginning to curl around the ends — as he sighed. "I suppose it is none of my business. And yet," he turned to face her now, his face twisted, "I hate to think of you resorting to such a thing, Juliet."

"Oh, do you?" she asked, the familiar ache of pain turned anger beginning to coil in her belly. "Perhaps you should have thought of that before you left me. Alone. Told that you wanted nothing more to do with me. That I should find my own way in life. Left, without anyone to care for me or see after me, recovering from a wound that was inflicted during one of your schemes."

And with a heart that was so broken she had thought that she would never recover.

"Exactly," Xander said, holding out a hand as if that was to explain everything, "you were hurt. And I didn't want you ever to be so hurt again."

"Very well," Juliet said, her shoulders dropping as the fight left her, and suddenly she was just tired. Tired and ready to move on from this. Ready to never see him again. She could only pray that he had been hired for this one night alone, for she didn't think she could continue to see him day in and day out. "You left. I've moved on. Our lives have gone their separate ways. I just need to know something, Xander."

"Of course."

"Are you just here for this party?"

Xander scratched his head in that way of his that she had always found most endearing, and she steeled her resolve against him.

"I'm here for... awhile. Until we find what we are here for."

"Which is?"

"Ah... I'm not sure I can say."

"Of course you can't." She crossed her arms over her chest in an attempt to shield herself from him as dread began to grow deep in her belly. "I must change and return to the party," she said, even as she wondered where Annabelle was. "You should go. You might be missed."

"Juliet," he said in supplication, and she lifted her brows, inviting him to say something, anything. To apologize for the past, to tell her that he had made the biggest mistake of his life. To plead for her forgiveness and explain that he was here because he had to find her again and make everything right. Because he still loved her.

And when he said all of that, she would laugh. Because she would never forgive him. Never. He had hurt her far too greatly.

Her imaginings were just that, however — imaginings. It was as she thought. He had nothing to say. No explanation. No excuse. She walked across the room and wrenched the door open, holding it for him in a sign that it was time for him to leave. He lowered his head in resignation as he walked toward it, pausing in the frame, inches away from her. "I'm sorry," he said, and then continued down the hall.

Juliet shut the door behind him, leaning her head against it.

She was sorry too. For she knew that as much as she told herself otherwise, she had never gotten over him. And she knew that, despite her best intentions, she never would.

* * *

?? Is now available on Amazon and in Kindle Unlimited.

ALSO BY ELLIE ST. CLAIR

Thieves of Desire
The Art of Stealing a Duke's Heart

For a full list of all of Ellie's books, please see www.elliestclair.com/books.

ABOUT THE AUTHOR

Ellie has always loved reading, writing, and history. For many years she has written short stories, non-fiction, and has worked on her true love and passion -- romance novels.

In every era there is the chance for romance, and Ellie enjoys exploring many different time periods, cultures, and geographic locations. No matter when or where, love can always prevail. She has a particular soft spot for the bad boys of history, and loves a strong heroine in her stories.

Ellie and her husband love nothing more than spending time at home with their two sons and Husky cross. Ellie can typically be found at the lake in the summer, pushing the stroller all year round, and, of course, with her computer in her lap or a book in hand.

She also loves corresponding with readers, so be sure to contact her!

www.elliestclair.com
ellie@elliestclair.com

Ellie St. Clair's Ever Afters Facebook Group

Printed in Great Britain
by Amazon